THE DRAGON ON THE FLAG

Dear Sharon,
Enjoy your Birthday Present!
P/ (Author & Friend of Mel)

Published by New Generation Publishing in 2021

Copyright © Paul Harries-Holt 2021

First Edition

The author asserts the moral right under the Copyright, Designs and Patents Act 1988 to be identified as the author of this work.

All Rights reserved. No part of this publication may be reproduced, stored in a retrieval system or transmitted, in any form or by any means without the prior consent of the author, nor be otherwise circulated in any form of binding or cover other than that which it is published and without a similar condition being imposed on the subsequent purchaser.

ISBN 978-1-80031-255-5

www.newgeneration-publishing.com

New Generation Publishing

Dedicated to

My Mother and Father.

Janice and Brian.

"Because of them this story came in to being"

To

John.

Mark.

David.

Iris.

In your honour and memory

Dear Sharon,

A little bit late for your birthday but hope you enjoy reading it.

Happy Belated Birthday!

Love Lots,

Mel xxx

01·05·2021

CHAPTERS

CHAPTER 1. The Story of Lucan

CHAPTER 2. The Story of Hazel

CHAPTER 3. The Story of Mark

CHAPTER 4. The Story of Quintus Antistius

CHAPTER 5. The Kingdom

CHAPTER 6. The Lady

CHAPTER 7. The Cooks Husband

CHAPTER 8. A Call to War

CHAPTER 9. The Northern Queen

CHAPTER 10. The lady and her story

CHAPTER 11. The Meeting of my Kin

CHAPTER 12. The Dig

CHAPTER 13. The Fall of a Kingdom

CHAPTER 14. The Story of Iris

CHAPTER 15. Princess Elizabeth

CHAPTER 16. The Promise

CHAPTER 17. The End?

Welcome reader.

It would seem you have chosen today of all days to pick up this book. Maybe you should ask yourself why today of all days you have chosen today - is it a Thursday afternoon and it's raining outside or is it a Sunday and you have put your tablet away for the first time all morning?

Could it be that curiosity has got the better of you? Or could it be, like so many before you, that you have a taste for legends and untold stories?

Whatever it is, you are welcome. You are about to start a journey that spans thousands of years of history. We will delve into pre-history, to a time before there were countries and even to a time before the last ice age when things and people were very different to what we know today.

Before we go on I feel it is very important to point out that some people think that they can pick up a newspaper or put on the television and be told why things are the way they are in our world. They are given an explanation and that's that forever. But the world is not like that. Things have lots of explanations, only a lot of people seem to take the most boring and dull of explanations and believe them, but I have a feeling that you are not like that?

For example have you ever stopped to think why there are seven days in a week? Why not six? or ten? Or why have we only two eyes and not three? Some questions are easy to answer, some questions only have one answer and some have lots. Indeed some cannot be answered at all. Some answers are simply another person's opinion. Whatever the question, it's very important that we ask it, for the pursuit of knowledge must always begin with one statement and that is "I do not know." From there you have no limits, and from there you can go anywhere and do anything if only you put your mind to it.

Have you ever wondered for example why there is a picture of a red dragon on the national flag of Wales?

A lot of people just take it for granted that a red dragon is there on the flag, with a background of white and green. Some people think the white and green are in fact the sky and the grass, but of course we know that isn't true, don't we?

Why is it that the Welsh flag looks so different to every other flag in the world? Indeed there are only two other national flags in the world that depict a Dragon: the mountainous kingdom of Bhutan and the flag of Malta too has a representation of a dragon upon it.

It may be small but it's definitely there if you take the time to look.

Of course there are dragons on other flags such as the city of Moscow flag, and the flag of Atlanta, Georgia USA and others however there are only three "Dragon flags" that actually represent a country.

The story you are about to read will explain why there is a dragon on the Welsh flag. It won't however be the official version or the version you will read on the Internet, or what you learnt in school no for this tale gives you a different version, one that starts a very long time ago in a world that is very different in so many ways to our world of today. Yet one thing is the same today as it was thousands of years ago and that is the hunger for stories, for women and men have always told stories. From the great folk tales of old, told only by word of mouth and passed down the years by those just like me and you who understand the importance of keeping our stories alive and kicking, to great story tellers such as Charles Dickens and Charlotte Bronte who have shaped our imagination. Some stories are dark and leave us feeling a little cold inside, and some fill our hearts.

Whatever the story, one thing is for sure: after we have read them or indeed heard them we are never quite the same again.

The first part of the story begins long ago in Wales but take heed this isn't just an ordinary story book but a collection of stories and eye witness accounts with poems written by people you may not know yet but you soon will and the more you read the stories, the more you will link each story together for yourself in the best legend maker of all - the human mind.

Chapter 1
The story of Lucan

It's a sunny, but somewhat windy day. The year is 1014 in southern Wales, and a poor but reasonably educated peasant is sitting alone under an oak tree near his home. It's mid-September. From where he is sitting, he can look out over the sea and just make out the Ogmore River that's been snaking its way through the sand dunes and mud flats for miles on its relentless journey to the sea, as it has done for centuries right up until this very day. Across the sea in the cloudy distance he can make out the far off cost line of what was then called Dyfneint in the land of Englaland upon which he has never set foot (but always wanted to) for this land was linked to his own by land and the day would come when both lands would become one, and then part of a United Kingdom with the great lands of the fair north, and across the sea to the west, and to a land that the old Roman empire called Hibernia.

For now, however, this island is full of small kingdoms, peoples and different languages and its ancient peoples have lived here for a very long time just like our peasant friend.

Should he look behind, he would be looking out over a green field and just beyond that a dirt track that steps three times gently up the hillside near his home.

A cloaked woman holding a long wooden staff is walking slowly down the rough track. She is tall, and her eyes are sky blue.

She is wearing a simple grey hooded robe, and she has a silver ring with a white stone on the second finger of her right hand. She is as much part of this ancient land as the Oak tree under which our peasant friend is now sitting.

She stops for a moment half way down and looks over at him under the tree, smiles and walks on whispering to herself "and so it begins."

He doesn't see her of course, as she walks on in to the distance and completely out of sight down what the local people call Three Step Hill.

It was said that long ago a knight chased a dragon across the fields here, and its feet pushed hard into the ground before it took to flight, escaping its determined pursuer and in doing so created indentations in the ground. But of course this was just a legend....

This isn't the first or last time the woman will come this way. Indeed she is no stranger to this part of South Wales and knows it as well as anyone who lives here today in the 21st Century.

Our peasant friend has met this woman before just three days ago in fact, when she came to his house looking to buy milk from his only cow. To him she seemed uninterested in the price of the milk, but instead wanted to engage him in conversation about the area and his family.

She asked him who owned the land and he told her that his great-grandfather, a John Lucan, had built the one storey stone house.

The house wasn't very big, and at the front were two windows and in the middle the front door.

Nailed upon the door was a small ancient plate of iron which was roughly engraved with a crown, and just underneath that was what looked to be the image of a quill. It was very old and its meaning was long forgotten by its owner. That was not surprising as it dates back to a time when South Wales was a very different place.

Lucan went on to tell her how the land had been in his family for as long as anyone could remember and that it had been handed down to him from his father and mother.

He owned the stone house and farmyard now, as well as the field where the great oak tree stood.

He told her that his father was a romantic and liked to tell unbelievable stories. He gave a little laugh and told her that his late father used to say his family were the descendants of a Princess whose father ruled this land long ago and it was part of the most prosperous kingdom on this old island but he did not believe such things. Although he did not live in grinding poverty he did not live in a great castle like his ancestors once did, as his father would have had him believe!

To this the lady told him that he should take the time to write those stories down some day, because there is nothing more important than keeping a record of stories.

Stories can of course tell us a lot about the past but they can shape the future in ways we cannot imagine. As they spoke her beautiful eyes for a brief moment closed, and without even buying any milk she smiled, turned and walked away towards the gate of the farmyard.

As she arrived at the small wooden gate she stopped to examine the oblong stone gatepost. It was standing upright, and two iron hinges had been hammered into it to attach a wooden gate. Along the entire length of it there was some writing. It was aged with time but more or less readable. Our peasant friend, who was left standing in the yard feeling slightly irritated at not making a sale of the milk, and extremely confused by what the woman said, was watching her as she ran her hand over the gatepost and using her finger she followed the lettering.

He joined her at the farmyard gate, looking at her with great interest. She turned and asked him where it had come from. He explained that when he was a boy he and his father had travelled to the monastery at Llandaff, some 25 miles away to the east, to buy some seedlings from the monks. On their way home, they stopped at the bank of the river Taff so the horse could take a drink and they saw the oblong stone in the mud of the riverbank. He went on to explain how his father was looking for such a stone to use as a gatepost.

He remembered the great weight of it as he and his father lifted it onto the cart and brought it home with them and here it had stayed ever since as a convenient gatepost. He had no idea how it came to be in the river and never really gave it much thought.

He looked at the woman as she stared at the stone and said "Lady, do you still wish to buy some milk from me?" She looked up from the stone and it was as though she hadn't heard his question and said in a quiet voice "Sir, can you read the writing here upon this stone?"

He stared at her and without thinking, said in an irritated voice "of course I can lady! It is in good Welsh! There are three words and they read LOVE THE LAND!" (His tone was somewhat frustrated as he felt the lady had deliberately ignored his question about the milk) She looked at the stone again and said almost to herself "of course it does, I did not expect to find this here." She smiled and turned to him. "Sir I no longer require any milk, but thank you very much indeed for your time this day." She made a small bow and left.

Our peasant friend was feeling even more confused, but now with a burning ambition to write out one of his father's stories (he had the ability to read and write, having been taught to do so by a local priest who had been friends with his late father) for her advice about the importance of writing down old stories seemed to have had a profound effect on him, and that is precisely what he did three days later under that tree. And so we return to him under that very tree for his story is the foundation of what's to come.

His somewhat scruffy appearance is matched only by the lingering odour that comes with the fact that showers, baths, and indeed soap have not been invented yet!

His name is Lucan, the name having been passed down to him from his great-grandfather. We don't know how old he was on that day in late summer, when he wrote down a tale in old Welsh, using a quill made from swan feathers and written on a piece of parchment (both of which he kept in a small box made from wood and metal that he had made when he was a boy) He also had a small silver inkwell that his father had left him that also just about fitted inside the box.

His story that has been translated several times over the centuries to what we know now is a tale that has fascinated people of all ages just like us ever since, and has been the bedrock for hundreds of other stories from that day to this.

The story he wrote down that day was told to him by his father years before. We can only assume that he had a great love for legends and myths to remember the story in the first place.

Here is Lucan's tale......

It came to pass that the Prince of South Wales and Uther Pendragon forced an enormous dragon into a great pit on Caerphilly mountain in South Wales. But Uther betrayed the Prince, and he was killed in a great battle defending the Welsh people from the marauding Anglo-Saxons.

Lucan's short story ends here and very little more is known about it or of Lucan - we can only assume that if he intended to add to the story he did not intend for anyone to read it. The only things we do know are his name, the year he put quill to parchment, the date and, of course, the location.

It has been translated from old Welsh into English (as well as other languages) over the years.

I am sure you will agree that it's a story of daring, courage and bitter betrayal- it also annoyingly leaves us with lots of questions.

Why did they capture the Dragon?
How did they do it?
Why did Uther betray the Prince?
How did his father know the story?

And probably most importantly- dragons don't exist, do they?

Surely then, this story is little more than a local legend?

I know what you are thinking: how after all those years do we know of that story? Well, there is a reasonable explanation, and it is because of what the peasant Lucan did with that short story after he had written it down.

There are a lot of conflicting theories about it, but most people do agree that he left it, along with everything he owned, to the Church, which tells us a little bit more about him and we may suppose that he had no living relatives at the time of his death.

One of the mysteries, however, is the fact that around 75 years after his death, the Church where some of his belongings ended up (about ten miles from his home) well and truly burnt to the ground. There has never been an explanation as to how this happened, but we do have an eyewitness account from a French monk, who was sent to what was left of the Church by William of Normandy (who by this time was King of England and most of Wales) to investigate and to see if any of the precious religious icons had survived the great fire.

The letter he sent back to the King still survives and has been translated from old French into modern English...

"Gracious sovereign,

I humbly wish to inform you that very little survived the great fire of the church in Glamorgan. Of the religious icons and treasures of the altar, alas, most have been destroyed; although somewhat damaged by the fire the wooden carving of the dragon that stood just inside the door way is much preserved.

Please see the list of what could be salvaged on the next page. I humbly beseech you, my Lord sovereign, that you commission the building of a new church.

My King, I must also mention the charity of one woman with eyes as blue as the sky, that offered to aid the sick and the poor of the area that depended on the church for help and in return has only asked for a small box

made of wood and metal that too survived the great fire; that only contained a few lines of text in the ancient Welsh language that I could not understand, along with a rather small inkwell and tattered quail.
May God bless her for her charity and generosity for such little reward.
Your humble and obedient servant,

Friar Vouiver"

Thanks to the good Friar, we know that a small fragile box survived the great fire and we know that the "few lines of text in the ancient Welsh language" was indeed the story that Lucan wrote years before was inside; that it was given as a reward to a kind and gracious woman for showing unbelievable generosity to those in need, however, whom that woman was or what she did with the box and the piece of parchment still remains (for the moment) unknown and it doesn't explain how it made it all the way to the 21st century and over 200 years pass until there is any hint of what may have happened to it.

Chapter 2
The Story of Hazel

We now leave Wales altogether and fast forward in time over 200 years from the time of Lucan and to the city of London where we will find a woman in the year 1231.

It is a turbulent time in England: there is unrest, war and plague, but even during the darkest times in history there is a glimmer of hope and light and it exists in a very unlikely place. I would ask you please to imagine a small house on the outskirts of the old city, with only two rooms next to each other. Made of wood with a thatched roof, it's nothing remarkable - in fact if you found yourself walking past it back then you would see a rundown little place with very little to offer, with its shabby front door and dirty windows. In one room is a homemade bed with an old wooden frame and a straw mattress and little else apart from a low set window looking out over a small shabby garden but on the wall above the bed there is something of interest: a wooden plaque with a faded wood carving of an open book, and a little crown just above it. It may have been some kind of ancient coat of arms but what or who it represents has been long forgotten, but this object is very special and indeed treasured by the occupant of this house.

Through the window you can see there is a small pig pen that used to house a pig but no more, and it's been allowed to fall into disrepair; its occupant long since sold off to make ends meet.

In the other room is a rackety unvarnished table and chair next to an open fire over which there is an ancient black pot babbling away and cooking up a dull vegetable pottage.

In the home made chair is our Hazel but to the people that know her she is The Widow Hazel, her husband having been killed two years before. Having been a soldier in the King's army, he was killed in battle, and now she is alone in this world - she has no children and no living relatives at all.

As she sits at the wooden table looking out over a cold January day she reads a poem partly from the paper in front of her, and partly from memory. It is something she had written two years before; as even before she was married she knew how to read and write for her mother thought it important that her only daughter should have the ability to read and write for her mother too was intelligent and had the ability to write beautiful poetry. Hazel was indeed extremely proud of it, for not many woman and girls of that time and station had this extremely precious gift. Yes, perhaps in a distant future all people would be given the opportunity to read and write, but for now it was extremely rare to meet a woman such as her with this remarkable gift.

Her poem is possibly the only thing she has left of any value. She is intending to take it to the Royal Court to present it to Queen Eleanor (the wife of King Henry III) for it is a well-known fact that Queen Eleanor has a great love of poetry and the arts.

Hazel has a burning ambition that her written work be recognised and appreciated by everyone and of course she also hopes that if the Queen likes her poem, she will reward her with some gold coins so at least she could replace the pig in the back garden.

Hazel is around 24 years old. She misses her husband for he was a good man; they met one day by chance in the market. His name was Aneroid. That name of course wasn't very common in London (or in England for that matter), for Aneroid was from the west - he was from South Wales and came to London when he was a boy to look for a better life, but ended up becoming a soldier.

Hazel fell for him instantly as they got talking in the market and a month later they were married. He was away on campaign a lot and one day he never came back, and Hazel knew she would never see him again. All she had left were her memories and the wooden plaque that her husband had made.

He told Hazel that he had often seen the symbol of the crown and the quill around his village, and many very old gravestones in his local graveyard had this symbol carved upon them but no one could really say why, and so the true origin of this mysterious symbol had been lost to time.

It now hung above her bed and she would kiss it each night before she slept.

Her husband spent many months teaching his wife how to speak Welsh and because of this Hazel could read and write in both English and Welsh. He also used to joke and say that the wooden plaque was his family crest, and that his family were the descendants of Welsh royalty from a time when South Wales was a prosperous and peaceful land, ruled over by princes and princesses who treated the people with respect and dignity.

He never really believed it, but he liked to talk about it. Most of his family history came from listening to stories from his mother and father before they both died of plague - he was left an orphan which was why aged only about 13 years old, he left Wales for London and a new life.

The city wasn't what we know London to be today- for a start it was a great deal smaller. Its people (for the most part) were poor and oppressed by anyone who was slightly richer than themselves; disease and injustice was everywhere; there was very little law and order, and on the outskirts of this mediaeval metropolis lived Hazel. If it wasn't for her poem, we wouldn't even know she ever existed but, as poor as she was, her life was about to change considerably for the better but not in the way she had expected or hopped.

So it came to the day that Hazel finally decided to visit the castle, and present her poem to the Queen. Her journey through the January snow to the castle was not an easy one. It was cold, and she found it long and difficult, but at last she made it to the gates of the great intimidating Tower fortress on the banks of the River Thames.

In front of the gates stood two battle hardened soldiers in heavy armour who looked upon her as if she was little more than a criminal. Suddenly she felt useless, undeserving and totally ridiculous. "Why," she thought to herself would the Queen be interested in her? Why would the Queen of the English want to read her poem when she had access to all the great writings the kingdom had to offer?

She was just about to turn and run away in disappointment and embarrassment when the taller of the two soldiers shouted, "State your business here woman!" On hearing those words, a fire of courage ignited within her and in her most courageous voice she said, "I am here to see the Queen, for I have a poem for her pleasure." The soldier looked at her with contempt. He sniggered but did not react in the way Hazel had expected (she had expected him to tell her extremely rudely to go away!) He simply said, "Wait here woman." He turned, opened the Great Gate and stepped inside, slamming it behind him.

The other soldier completely ignored her and stared straight ahead. The time passed- five minutes, ten minutes. She was very cold and began walking up and down in front of the Castle to try and keep warm. Then, without thinking, she looked up to a window set half way up the side of the Castle and just above it was a stone carving of a dragon's head. Like all the other gargoyles, it was there to encourage the rainwater away from the walls of the Castle, but in a window Hazel noticed a lady smiling down at her. She was extremely beautiful, in a green dress and cloak.

Hazel could see her hands, sitting one on top of the other neatly at her waist, and in the sun of the January day she could make out quite clearly a silver ring with a white stone on the second finger of her right hand.

Their eyes met for a brief moment then, without any warning, the rough voice of the soldier rang out like a broken bell, "You, woman! Come with me now!" She jumped as if coming out of a day dream. The bottom of her old cloak was extremely wet and her feet were freezing.

She reluctantly followed the soldier through the old studded oak doors into a courtyard; through another door and up some stone steps. At the top the soldier stopped and said in a gruff voice, "wait here" and he walked off back down the stone steps just as his footsteps were dying away the door opened and standing there was a young girl, a housemaid in a black gown.

She bowed Hazel through the door in to a room with great tapestries hanging from the walls, at one end a fire was burning in a large fireplace and the other was a window that was letting in the cold January light.

Hazel's eyes then turned to the middle of the room, where a fine tall woman was standing with two ladies-in-waiting on each side of her but standing slightly behind. She was in a green dress and cloak, her long hair in a tight plait resting over her right shoulder. Her eyes were a deep sky blue and she had a smile that suggested welcome and warmth and spoke first, "I understand, dear lady, that you have a gift for me- a poem no less." Hazel, unsure of what to say, gave a low curtsey, and simply said, "Yes, your Majesty," not daring to look this gracious lady in the eye.

"Then I would like you to please read it to me, for I always think the creator of the poem should be the first to read it out loud." The lady was looking directly at Hazel.

With shaking hands Hazel reached inside her cloak and brought out a piece of paper, aged with time and with slight tears around the edges. She unfolded it with a slight crackle of the paper and looking down she began to read in a quiet but steady voice,

"As the sun sets over our Britannic islands, the moon rises to hold dominion over our home, and with it comes all the mysteries of the night. For only in the darkness can we truly appreciate the primeval longing, and the delicate promise that the sun will rise again over Britannia. The feared Noctis will always be with us, like the grief at the loss of a loved one, but the sunlight will always prevail. Never lose hope that the light will always come and even in the darkness of night the sun will always rise again"

Anyone else who was standing in that room just then would surely understand that this poem was one of grief at the loss of someone near because grief, as we know, isn't exclusive, it affects each and every one of us. It can walk at our side, and sometimes be ignored and then jump out on us when we least expect it. To experience grief, first we must experience love, for love and grief walk together hand in hand. As our own beloved Queen Elizabeth II said, "Grief is the price we pay for love."

It is true that it is a price worth paying, because the absence of love is worse than grief - and I think Hazel felt this at that moment as she looked up from the paper and for the first time looked directly into the lady's face saying, "Your Majesty, I wrote that poem the day I knew that my dear husband had been killed in the service of the King. I also wrote it for the great love I feel for these old islands that I call my home."

The lady looked at Hazel and with a great deal of genuine sympathy she said the only thing that anyone can say in that situation (for words are never enough but sometimes they are all we have) "My dear lady, I am so, so sorry for your loss, now I would ask you to be of service to me. From your poem that I love a great deal I feel that you have a great love not only of writing, but of your country.
   The day may come when the sun may set on Britannia in a great fire, and should that day come all we want to build on in the centuries to come will be destroyed in arrogant aggression and flame."

The lady held out her right hand to the side and into it one of the ladies-in-waiting placed a scroll of parchment. "Take this, dear lady, and read it. Add a second verse in your own words and return here to me within five days with it and I will see that you want for nothing all the days of your life."
   Those words fascinated and terrified Hazel at the same time.

She took the paper from the lady; It too was aged with time, so to protect it she put it inside her cloak.

Hazel, feeling rather perplexed as she was hoping for a few gold coins to replace the pig in her back garden, said "of course Your Majesty, but don't you have great scholars at your command that could do a much better job then I?"

To this the lady smiled and simply said "I wish you to do it.
    Now please leave for your home and return to me in five days time with the second chapter and you will be rewarded most handsomely."

Then, before Hazel could gather her thoughts, the housemaid that had opened the door to her came forward from a dark corner and was this time showing her out. But Hazel stopped, turned, and gave a low curtsey to the lady then left the room. She went down the stone staircase, through the door into the courtyard and then out in to the snow again. The old oak doors being opened by the same intimidating soldier that had let her in not 20 minutes before hand. She felt somewhat disappointed at leaving with only a roll of paper, but felt resolute that she would carry out the Queen's wishes and return in five days time for her generous reward as promised by none other than the Queen of the English....

Hazel journeyed to her house through the snow and the cold until at least she made it to her front door. She went inside and fell upon her bed, sleeping soundly until morning. She completely forgot about the piece of parchment that the Queen had given her.

The next morning she woke up with a start and, remembering the parchment and the promise of a great reward, in the early cold morning Hazel sat at the table and unfolded the piece of parchment and began to read.

The writing was not very clear and had faded with time and was in the Welsh language, but this of course did not prevent her from reading it for she could read both English and Welsh….

It came to pass that the Prince of South Wales and Uther Pendragon forced an enormous dragon into a great pit on Caerphilly mountain in South Wales….

She read it to the very end and then laughed out loud! And said to herself "Why on earth would the Queen want me to add to such nonsense? This is but a children's story of myth and legend!"

Why would a great Queen be interested in all of this? Her laughing soon stopped when a branch from a great tree that stood next to her house fell, hit and smashed the window in her bedroom! The great crash made her jump up and run to the bedroom! She began to cry because she knew she had no money to repair the window and she would surely freeze to death! Feeling a great deal of determination she sat at the table, took up her quill and began to write the following words in English.

As she wrote something inside her told her that she had heard this story before but she couldn't remember where and even if she did- it was more like a memory or dream long ago when she was a child.....

"Uther never told anyone exactly where the Dragon was imprisoned and took the secret with him to his grave.

Before he too was killed he asked the witch Morgana to put a spell on the mountain so that the dragon would never be discovered - but dragons can live forever. Many people have dedicated their lives searching for it over the last 1000 years but no one has been able to find it and many have gone mad in its pursuit."

When she had finished Hazel put down her quill and smiled. It had been a long time since she had heard the name Uther Pengragon and had never been to Wales - the birth place of her late husband but Morgana she had indeed heard of, for all the English, Welsh, Scottish and Irish knew that name.

For she is the greatest sorcerer of legend, she must be feared and loved at the same time, but Hazel knew that it was only a story. But also she felt sure that the Queen would too have heard of her, and that is why (in part) she added Morgana to her part of the story. She sat back in her chair and closed her eyes. In her mind's eye she could see her mother's face. She was talking to her but the words she could not hear but she suddenly realised it wasn't the first time she had been told this story but she could not remember for sure who had told her? Maybe it was her mother but she would never know for sure, only that it was an echo of a memory from when she was very young.

The snow was lying heavy across London and the widow Hazel slammed her front door shut. Pulling her cloak over her head she began walking and making her way to see the Queen. She walked past all kinds of people in the crowded London streets: soldiers, merchants, monks and every day folk just like her. Some said hello but Hazel, with her head down walking in a straight line barely noticed them. All she could think about was the reward that the Queen has promised her. It is the fifth day and she is due at the Castle to present her part of the "childish" legend to Queen Eleanor, consort to King Henry III, King of England, Lord of Ireland and Duke of Aquitaine. Her last visit was confusing to say the least, however she has now completed her task and now it was time to be rewarded. As she approached the gates of the fortress she could see the same soldier guards. As she walked nearer the same soldier held up his hand and said "Come in woman you are expected." Feeling relieved Hazel followed the soldier again through the great gates, through the courtyard and up the stone steps to the door leading to the Queens chamber. Again the door opened and there in the middle of the room was the same lady, this time in a beautiful red gown but with the same silver ring with a white stone on her finger. Hazel curtsied and the lady smiled and said "My dear woman, have you completed your task?" to which Hazel replied "Yes Your Majesty" and from under her damp cloak she took the piece of parchment and held it out to the lady. The lady-in-waiting to her left took it and put it in to a small box made from metal and wood and left the room. This confused Hazel but before she could speak the lady held up her right hand in a gesture that suggested silence and said "Thank you for carrying out this task and for coming to me on the fifth day. You have done well, now you must be rewarded." Hazel's heart jumped in her chest and all she could think about was getting a new pig! The lady continued

"…From this day forward you will not want for anything for a gold sovereign will be brought by special messenger to you each month." Hazel could not contain her joy at this news for she was indeed a poor widow and exclaimed "Thank you! Thank you, gracious Queen!" To this the lady replied "No, my good woman, thank you.

For you have indeed played your part in saving this kingdom of ours from a terrible threat of fire and arrogance. Leave now and enjoy your reward for you deserve it."

Hazel made a very low curtsey, stood up, walked backwards five paces and was about to turn but instead began to speak: "Gracious sovereign, you did not read the.... but the lady interrupted her, smiled and said "dear lady, I have no need to read it until it is completed and it is far from being so and there is but one more thing I must tell you before you leave this day…"

Before saying anymore she clapped her hands and the ladies-in-waiting left the room leaving Hazel and the lady quite alone. Hazel did not move or say anything but just stood looking at the lady.

The lady then took both Hazel's hands in hers and said "I know it will come as surprise to you but I am indeed not the Queen of the English. I am but a visitor to this city. I know that I led you to believe I was a queen and why I did this is not important but you must trust me, the real Queen is in France with the King and I am but a guest here in this fortress. All I have asked of you and all that I have said is for the greater good of this country and its people now and in the future, for this land is part of me and I love it so. Because of that I ask you now to please trust me and do not speak of this to anyone.

Now leave this place and return to your home and as I promised a gold sovereign will be delivered to you each month for as long as you live."

Hazel smiled somewhat confusingly and left the room. She did what the lady asked of her and did indeed return to her home.

In the months and years to come Hazel lived a happy life. She bought two pigs, fixed her window and lived to a great age, for the lady whom she had met in the Castle kept her promise and Hazel did indeed receive a gold sovereign every month but she never saw who delivered it. Sometimes she would find it on her door mat in the morning, or slipped in to her basket when she was shopping in the market but no one ever put it in to her hand.

From time to time she thought she saw the lady from the castle but did not know for sure, because it was only ever out of the corner of her eye in the street, or in church on a Sunday

Hazel, however, never forgot that strange encounter and what the lady had said to her.....

"Thank you for you have indeed played your part in saving this kingdom of ours from a terrible threat of fire and arrogance…" Hazel never really understood what that meant and she never knew the true importance of it.

Chapter 3
The Story of Mark

The year is 1509 and over 270 years have passed since Hazel's visit to the great fortress in London.

A boy of just 18 years of age is making his way from the coast up through England, to the small town of Bath, for he has been told of the healing properties of the water found there.

He is an honest lad, hard-working and polite, dressed in a pair of leather shoes, some trousers that are a little too short for him, a loose fitting shirt and a straw hat. He has with him a small leather bag that he borrowed from his father for the journey. He has very few personal belongings but around his neck on the end of a piece of string is a bronze disc (about the size of a modern two penny piece.) It's very old and engraved into it is a musical note and above that a crown. It is very precious to him because his grandmother gave it to him for his tenth birthday and she made him promise that he would never take it off. He didn't know where she got it from and he never got the chance to ask her because she died just days after his birthday but his father told him that it had something to do with his ancient Welsh ancestors.

It is an exciting time for soon England will have a new King. The kingdom is all a buzz talking about Henry Tudor, the young man that is to be crowned King of all England and Wales in just two days time.

There is optimism in the air and in each town and village our traveller passes through there are preparations for the up and coming coronation. Flags and bunting of white and green are strung from the wooden houses of the towns and the people are preparing great feasts to celebrate this momentous occasion, for a coronation is in a way a nations birthday and worthy of a great celebration across the land.

The Traveller whose name is Mark, however, is not interested in such matters. For him street parties and the drinking of ale are of no importance for he has one thing on his mind and that is to take the waters at Bath. His journey from his home is a long one as he has no horse so must travel on foot only, but he is fit and healthy with no physical ailments, he comes from a family of blacksmiths in Portsmouth that are relatively well off, and although Mark is illiterate he is by no means stupid.

He is three days in to his journey to Bath. The food he brought with him has now run out but he's not at all concerned because from the hill top where he is sitting to rest he can see a village. He knows that he can indeed find food and rest there. He has no money but will quite literally sing for his supper for in his home town he is considered to have a great singing voice so he is intending to sing his way in to the good books of the people in that village in exchange for a meal or two and maybe even a room for the night.

Smiling to himself he stands and stretches in the midday sun and makes his way down in to the village some three miles away.

Just as he gets to the village boundary, he can hear a lot of noise and commotion. In the distance he can just make out several people: some are heaving great sacks of what was probably grain on to the back of a small horse drawn cart that stood in the village square, surrounded by white houses with black beams. Children are running around shouting and screaming with joy, some people are in the process of hanging out dull but coloured flags of white and green from their windows, others are busy with various tasks such as laying out great long tables in preparation of what looks to be a modest yet exciting celebration to welcome a new king to the throne.

For the past ten years things have not been easy for the people and now with the promise of a new young king there is much to be optimistic about.

As Mark made it to the centre of the village some heads turned to look at him. A woman who was laughing because her husband had fallen out of a downstairs window while trying to hang a flag suddenly stopped laughing and stared at Mark. Others were whispering to each other "Who is this boy?" and "Do we know his family?"

The people of the village were not used to strangers just walking in to their village square and this young man was definitely not part of their community.

That's not to say, however, that they didn't welcome strangers. Indeed just a week before, a lone woman on horseback had arrived to ask directions. She was indeed memorable because not only was it unusual for a woman to be travelling alone in those days, but she seemed to be out of place. Some of the women of the village did comment with slight envy on a beautiful silver ring with a white stone that the stranger was wearing on her finger and no one could really pinpoint her accent to any region. But if you were to ask the villagers why this woman with beautiful blue eyes seemed unusual not one of them could really give you a satisfactory answer- only that she stayed for a few hours and then left heading north, but not before handing a small purse of money to the village magistrate on the proviso that it be used only for their coronation celebrations. The magistrate kept to the agreement and used the silver coins to purchase food and drink for all the villagers in preparation for the planned party.

Mark is used to the reaction he received from the villagers as he had encountered it in every village and hamlet he passed though since he started his journey.

The magistrate, who was supervising three men rolling barrels of ale across the square to a secure location next to his house, stopped too and eyed the traveller with mild suspicion. Then, making sure the barrels were in place, walked over to the boy and said in a somewhat nervous, high-pitched voice "Good afternoon my boy. I am John, the Town Magistrate and chief organiser of the up-and-coming celebrations to mark the coronation of our new King."

Before Mark could give any kind of answer to this statement, however, a plump woman with a blotchy red face came hurrying over to the magistrate and in a deep breathless voice declared "Sir, old Ned is upon his bed sick with fever! He no doubt cannot rise to sing at the celebration!" She was bent forward with her hands upon her knees, panting with despair and disappointment!

To this Mark smiled to himself but remained silent and John the magistrate looked just as disappointed as the breathless woman who broke the news of Ned! "Janet are you sure of this? Could it be that old Ned has been at his own moonshine again for it would not be the first time he has over done it!" Janet, by now standing upright and slightly less breathless, spent the next five minutes telling John the magistrate, Mark and a small group of people who had gathered around to listen to how old Ned was absolutely fine the day before when he was collecting apples in the orchard, but now is sick with a high fever and not able to sing at the village party!

John, the Magistrate, spoke first and said "My dear friends, do not be dismayed, for I am sure we can find another singer of songs in time." The villagers just looked at him with suspicion and mistrust. The only person in the village that could hold a note was old Ned! He had been singing at special occasions in the village for as far back as most people could remember, and he was unwell and not able to do so this time! To this Mark saw his opportunity! Suddenly, and without thinking, he ran forward jumped onto one of the long tables that had been laid out and began to sing!

> *"O ' English land*
> *Come hither and band*
> *Together to sing and rejoice.*
> *For a King will be crowned*
> *To erase every frown*
> *And give every peasant a voice.*
> *Come on kind Sir and have drink!"*

The villagers stood with their mouths open listening to the singing voice of a boy who was a great stranger. When he had finished singing there was a brief pause that was met with great cheering and clapping from all the people of the village!

The magistrate, John, stepped forward just as Mark jumped down from the table. Taking him by the hand he said "My boy if you are willing to sing at our coronation celebrations the day after tomorrow I will give you permission to stay in the village for as long as you wish, to eat and drink with us!"

To this Mark agreed and was shown to a small but comfortable room in the town's only public house where there was a bed and some ancient furniture.

As darkness fell and after a great deal of drinking and feasting, he faced a great many questions from the villagers as to why he had left his home (and the celebrations that would no doubt be held in Portsmouth too) to travel alone on foot to Bath, to which our traveller didn't really give an answer to the kind yet very inquisitive people of the town.

At one in the morning, and feeling sleepy, Mark returned to his room. For most people the prospect of a warm comfortable bed after a long day's travel is a welcome sight, but for this boy there is no rest in sleep. For him the prospect of a good night's sleep brings with it a feeling of dread. Though he is in physically good health he experiences something each night that most of us just dismiss as nothing more than an over worked imagination, for every time he falls asleep he has the same nightmare and has done since the day of his tenth birthday.

It is the same each time, and without exception leaves him feeling cold inside when he awakes in the morning- that feeling we all have when we wake from a nightmare, but for him it has been every night since he was ten years old and he knew that tonight would be no exception.

After taking a drink of water and gets in to bed a part of him feels happy and proud of his actions in the Village that day but as he begins to drift off to sleep he knows what is coming and there is nothing he can do to stop it.....

It always starts with the same thing. He can hear a voice in the darkness - he can never decide if it's the voice of a man or a woman.

It's a far away voice - nowadays we would perhaps describe it as to the likes of trying to hear someone speaking on a mobile telephone when they are going through a tunnel or when you are trying to hear a song on the car radio when you drive out of range of the radio station on a long car journey and it is the same words over and over:

"The centuries will pass and the people will say that they can hear the dragon roaring deep inside the Mountain!"

Then the same disturbing scenes start to play over and over again!

He can see a mountain and nearby a town but not any kind of town he has ever seen before. The buildings look alien to him. Very little of this town looks familiar.

There are tall buildings that look as if they are shining with glass. There are strange shaped things in many different colours moving along black roads.

The strangely dressed people of the town are speaking English amongst other languages but he can't understand a lot of the words. He sees a ruined castle in the middle of the town and the voice starts again....

"Take heed! For when Morgana's spell is all but ended and when the old ways of Magic are completely forgotten by the Welsh people, the dragon will break free of the mountain and take its revenge on all Britain"

Mark is then subjected to terrible scenes of a great winged monster bursting out of the side of a mountain with eyes as red as fire! It flies over the town breathing its fire in every direction; there is screaming and devastation right across the town and then all across the entire kingdom!

When Mark awakes in the morning he is feeling upset and cold inside because again he had the same nightmare!

He allows himself to wake up properly.

He doesn't recognise the area in his dream, he doesn't know where it is, he knows of no ruined castle surrounded by a strange town, but the one thing he does know and that is the name Morgana, for she is as much part of the island he lives on as the birds in the trees and the rabbits in the fields. She is a being of great power and legend, her name is known to all that live here.

After ten minutes he sits up and gets out of bed knowing that when he goes back to sleep that evening it will all begin again! "Maybe," he thinks to himself "when I reach Bath and take the waters all of this will end and I will dream of better things."

His day is spent with the villagers, preparing for the great feast the following day. There is much to do and he is kept busy fetching and carrying. By late afternoon he finally has time to sit and prepare his songs that he intends to sing the following day. Although he has no aptitude for the written word, he has a very good memory. He remembers the songs his mother and two sisters would sing on wash day, the songs the men would sing on the way home from the fields and the public house. He was looking forward to tomorrow. He planned to leave as soon as his singing was over, for as much as he enjoyed the festivities and the company of the villagers, he must reach Bath because for him nothing else mattered other than driving this nightmare from his mind and to at last have a peaceful night's sleep.

The following day he woke early again after experiencing the same repetitive nightmare. Within 30 minutes he had taken breakfast and was standing in the town square. It truly was a magnificent sight. Any rubbish there may have been lying about had been taken away and the town square looked truly beautiful for this was Coronation Day.

As the morning wore on, the people enjoyed all manner of entertainment from juggling to acrobats.

There was food and drink aplenty, and a good time had by all in celebration of the new King Henry the eighth: King of all England and Wales.

Even old Ned was feeling better and had a little to eat and drink with his friends.

Our travelling singer did a good job, and well and truly sang his heart out.

After his last song the magistrate John announced to all the people that he intended in way of gratitude and thanks to present Mark with a horse and as many provisions that he could carry. So at around two in the afternoon Mark began the rest of his journey to Bath, only this time not on foot but on a beautiful brown horse laden with food and drink and so, to much cheering, he rode out of the village on the last leg of his journey.

The sun was setting when, sitting on the brown horse, he finally reached the ancient town of Bath. He had heard all kinds of stories and tales about this place, and how long ago an empire started in what is now Italy spread right across to England, and even then those people knew how important the water was there. As he approached the ruined bathhouse he expected to find a great many people still celebrating the coronation, but there was nobody in sight. The town of Bath lay half a mile away from the ruins so he supposed that nobody had any use for the healing waters during a great celebration and indeed he was right. He was also pleased that he was alone as he didn't want any interruptions. He dismounted from the horse, and tied her reins securely to a nearby tree. Not without some apprehension, he walked towards the ruins, following the sound of running water.

As he approached the ruins he stopped and looked down at a part-ruined statue that looked a little like a dragon. It was lying on its side and it was part covered in moss, its face partly worn away by the weather and time. As he looked at the face of the mythical animal he heard footsteps behind him. He quickly turned around and standing in front of him was a tall beautiful woman, her hair loose over her shoulders, her eyes as blue as the sky.

She was dressed head to foot in a pale blue gown, holding a wooden staff and on her finger was a silver ring with a white stone. She smiled at him and any feeling of surprise and trepidation he may have felt simply faded away, for all he felt now was trust and calm. For a moment they both just looked at each other, the sun was almost set.

The lady spoke first. "Good evening to you young man"

I see you have been studying that ancient statue? It is indeed a dragon but a small and somewhat inaccurate interpretation I always think." Before Mark could make any kind of answer or even a greeting, the strange woman added "Why are you not in the town making merry with the towns people in welcoming the new King?" Her voice was light and at once he knew that this woman could be trusted. He answered and explained that he had come to Bath to take the waters because he had the most distressing nightmare every night and that he had been told that the water has healing properties not only for the body but also the mind and he hoped before the night was over he would be rid of it for good!

The lady listened to his every word and agreed with him that she too believed that the water would take away his nightmares. She recommended that he drink at once, so taking a wooden cup that the villagers had given him with a roughly painted green and white flag on one side, he dipped it in to the spring and took a deep long drink of the warm sweet water. It wasn't anything special, in fact it didn't taste very nice but that didn't stop him feeling a great deal of relief having at last done so. But he did not feel any different- although he wasn't sure what was going to happen after he had taken a drink, the only thing he felt was blind hope that the next time he slept he would not have the nightmare that had been plaguing him for years.

He turned and told the woman that he would now leave for the town and find a room for the night to sleep and find out if it had worked or not. Again to this the woman agreed and said it was in her opinion the best thing to do but added "Before you leave, young man, would you do me one great favour?" At this Mark became somewhat confused.

He had just assumed this woman was from the town and was simply on an evening stroll maybe to escape the noise and festivities from the town. What favour could he possibly do for her?

Not forgetting his manners he looked her directly in the face and said "Yes of course I will".

She smiled and said "You are a kind and thoughtful young man, would you please tell me about your nightmare and would you permit me to write it down?"

Mark was astonished at this request but did not question it. He simply thought she was a little eccentric, and maybe she did this kind of thing as a pastime or hobby so he simply replied "Yes of course madam." She put her hand inside her robe and brought out a small box made of wood and metal. Opening it, she brought out an old looking piece of parchment, a quill and a very small silver inkwell. She placed all three on to a giant piece of marble that looked as if it had once formed part of a gateway to the spring a very long time ago.

Kneeling in front of it and taking up the quill, she dipped it into the inkwell. Looking up at David she smiled to indicate she was ready. The boy looked down and saw there was more writing on the old role of parchment. Although he could not read it, he could tell it was written in at least two other hands and in a calm and quiet voice he told this complete stranger the story of his nightmare. As he spoke she wrote each word until he was finished. At that point the woman rolled up the parchment and placed it back in to the box, closed it and put it inside her robe. She then closed the lid of the inkwell and holding it out to Mark she said "Take this inkwell young man as payment and reward for sharing your nightmare with me. I know that it is in your nature not to expect it, but I ask you to please gracefully accept this along with this quill. Maybe in time you will learn to read and write and these tools will help you for the art of reading and writing is very important." Mark graciously took the inkwell and the quill and thanked the lady.

She stood up and said "Thank you young man.
Now go into the town where I am sure you will find a room for tonight. A truly magnificent thing has

happened this evening, and you dear boy have been part of it." Without another word the woman turned and walked away. Mark called after her and said "Lady do you live here?" Stopping, turning, and smiling, the lady said "Yes, dear boy. This land is my home and I have lived here for a very long time." Mark was a little confused by this answer, but did not comment. She then mounted a beautiful black horse that was grazing nearby and rode off into the darkness.

Mark was feeling incredibly confused by this encounter; he had never before told anyone the full, unedited tale of his nightmare. What, he thought to himself, made him do so, tonight of all nights and to a complete stranger? To this question the young man never really got an answer although it never really bothered him.

He smiled to himself, placed the inkwell and quill in to his leather bag, mounted his own horse and rode into the town where indeed he did find a room for the night. Later that night, he fell in to a deep sleep only this time and for the first time in eight years he dreamt only of a young girl his own age whom he loved and wanted to marry.

She was in his home town, and he missed her a great deal! In the morning after a light breakfast he leapt out of bed, jumped onto his horse, galloped out of the town of Bath, past the old ruins and the spring and headed south for Portsmouth.

We don't know anything more about him or what it was about the water that finally and completely took away the pain of the repetitive nightmare, but we can hope he made it safely home and did indeed marry his beloved.

As for the lady, we don't know where she went or what she did after meeting with Mark. The box, however, did turn up centuries later in the British Library in London in the early Victorian period. Could it be that the lady saw to it that this little box was kept safe, and then finally made its way in to the British Library centuries later? I think we can safely say that's exactly what happened don't you think so?

Chapter 4
The Story of Quintus Antistius

Now we step back in to the distant past, to a time long before the days of Lucan, Hazel and Mark.

The year is around 178AD for this story cannot be told without going back to a time when these islands were part of a great empire. For this story can only be truly understood if you know how and why it all happened. It starts with the sunrise on a cold morning in March, over 1800 years ago, in Northern England. There is a heavy damp mist resting across the land. Nothing is moving except a small mouse running along the side of a stone wall. Now if this small creature was to run the full length of this wall it would indeed run from one side of the land to another. This wall was built on the orders of a great Emperor from across the sea, and at this point in the past the wall is at its most effective and most used by all who live along it. We know a great deal about this wall and why it was built. Yes, great archaeological treasures have been found along it and it has been scrutinised and studied. However, what happened during that week in March will not show up in any academic history book. For that week long ago is shrouded in myth and legend but like every myth it is left to the reader to decide the truth.

As the sun penetrates its way through the mist, it begins to fade away to reveal a magnificent site that dominates the landscape, for nothing like this has been seen before in Britannia - a wall that marks the most northerly point of the Roman Empire!

It's a symbol of dominance and power on the island. Soldiers patrol it and families have made their home along it, ancient people live either side of it and each day people pass through it from one side to the other through stone gateways of forts that stand each mile or so apart along it. It is in one of them a man is just getting out of bed. His name is Quintus Antistius and he is the Roman Governor of Britannia. He is not a particularly good commander or soldier. He is, however, a good man. He of course puts the Empire before all things but he doesn't terrorise the people of Britannia. He is kind and generous which was unusual for the time. The only thing he loves more than the Empire is his wife. Her name is Fran and she is a good kind woman. They have no children and this makes them both very sad indeed but they are yet to give up hope that one day they will have a son or daughter.

After a wash and something to eat Quintus Antistius steps outside onto the small parade ground. He is feeling agitated for today he is due to meet with someone he has heard a great deal about. This person is coming to visit him and part of him just wants it over and done with.

He knows what the visitor wants but believing it is quite different. He is standing there in his toga, feeling very silly not to mention very cool, for this official costume would be more fitting in the warmer temperatures of the Mediterranean and not a cold March morning on a northern hillside.

Just then two soldiers came out carrying a smoking hot brazier and they set it down next to the governor and then taking their place each side of him they wait in the cold morning.

At 8 o'clock on the dot the gates of the wall fort open to let in all kinds of people. Most are native Britons. They come each day to deliver goods, to work and to generally serve the Roman garrison stationed there. There is much chatter and commotion with oxen pulling carts and all kinds of people doing all kinds of different things. There is shouting in different languages and a great deal of noise. There was nothing different about this, in fact each day would start like this and had done for many years.

Quintus Antistius is still waiting. The gates are about to close when through the smoke of the brazier he sees a tall woman walking through the arch way in to the parade ground with a wooden staff in her hand. She is wearing a simple grey cloak and dress and he knows at once this was the person who he was expecting. He had never seen her before but somehow he knew it was her. As she walked through the people and the commotion, none of it seemed to bother her. It was as if nobody even saw her. She came closer to him and finally spoke in fluent Latin "Good morning to you, my lord governor. Thank you very much indeed for seeing me today." Quintus Antistius simply looked at her, threw out his chest and tried to make himself look taller than her (it didn't work).

After a short time the lady smiled and said "Is there anywhere we could have a private conversation my Lord Governor?"

To this he answered, "Yes lady, follow me." Turning swiftly around he marched in to a small stone building. The two Roman soldiers followed and stood outside the door as the lady followed him inside. He gestured to her to sit and she did so on a hardback chair, and he remained standing. The room was where some of the soldiers took their meals. There were several chairs and a long wooden table. She made herself comfortable and with eyes as blue as the clear March sky she looked at him for some sign he was ready for their conversation. Moments passed and he didn't say a word, so feeling somewhat frustrated the lady spoke first. "Lord Governor, we have been corresponding by letter for some weeks. You have known of my coming for all that time but now it is as if I am a complete surprise to you." His eyes narrowed and a great smile burst upon his face. "Lady you are of course welcome here. I have been waiting for you in the cold of the morning. I know of course why you are here but I find what you ask for almost impossible, as I did point out in my letters. Indeed I have many requests from all kinds of people each day but nothing even comes close to what you are asking of me." The lady didn't seem moved by this statement. She simply sat quietly and listened and the governor continued "I know, of course, who you are and what you have done; the great lengths you have gone to in the mediation between the local people and the empire.

I know of all the help you have given not only to the native Britons that live here, but to the ordinary soldiers and their families. You have helped to heal the sick and help the poor but asked nothing in return." At this the lady smiled and said "my Lord Governor, all that I have done I did for the love I feel for all people, no matter where they come from. But the time has come for me to leave this place and travel to the south." The governor felt almost disappointment at this because he knew of all the good things she had done for all the people that lived along this vast wall. He would not show it but he would be sorry to see her leave.

The lady again made her request of the governor, a request she has been making for the last six weeks by letter. These letters that have been brought to him every other day by messenger from her home some 20 miles away to the east along the wall where she had built a small hospital and food supply station to help the poor people (Britain and Roman alike). Now it would close, and there would be no help for the people in this part of the Roman province of Britannia. This concerned him a great deal, for he was a good man and knew of the importance of the work this lady was doing. She did not change her composure but simply smiled at him. Moments passed and the governor began to pace up and down. His face looked to be deep in thought until at last he turned to the woman and said "if you can find a suitable replacement to administer the hospital and food station before you leave, I promise I will grant your request and give you what you ask for."

He almost shouted out the words because he knew there would be a great deal of legal loopholes to jump through to give her what she asked for, but in good conscience he could not let all the work she had done simply fade away. The lady smiled and said "yes, Lord Governor, I will do so. I will leave now and make the necessary arrangements and return here to you in three days for the written confirmation of your promise" and before he could gather his thoughts she stood up and swept out of the room, walked across the sandy parade ground, pushed open the gate and disappeared through it.

She made her way back along the Great Wall. It was a long way on foot but it did not bother her. She knew this land and its people very well. No one could say how long she had lived here or why she came, but come she did and did all she could to help anyone in need.

She was a skilled mediator and would help out in different legal and civil disputes amongst the people who lived along the wall. She was greatly respected by both the native Britons and the Romans. The governor of course knew this, and that was one of the reasons why he didn't want her to leave.

Two days passed and the governor set about making the arrangements for her return. He planned to leave Hadrian's Wall himself before the week was over for he had been here for some months and now it was time to travel to a different part of the province he governed on behalf of the Roman Empire for it wasn't prudent to stay in one place for too long.

He ordered that a document be written outlining the promise he had made as to cement the agreement he reluctantly made with this lady who had done so much for so many.

The document written in Latin was as follows:

I, Quintus Antistius,

Governor of the Imperial Roman province of Britannia, Commander of the ninth legion, senator of Rome.

Hereby grant the bearer of this Imperial Document full ownership of the mountain that stands seven miles from the sea and eight miles from the garrison headquarters in western Britannia superior.

This Imperial Deed of gift cannot and will not be contested on pain of death.

He signed the bottom and attached the official Roman seal with his own hands. It was of red wax and stamped with his personal emblem of a dragon.

He had absolutely no doubt that the lady would return. He knew in his heart that she too would keep her promise to find a suitable replacement to run and administer all that she had set up some 20 miles away for the good of all in need.

At precisely 8 o'clock in the morning on the third day the gates of the fort opened, only this time the expected lady was at the front of the many people who had come as they did every day with all manner of business and deliveries. The governor Quintus Antistius was standing in the same place but with no guards or smoking brazier, and this time he had a thick woolly cloak wrapped around him to keep out the cold.

He smiled as the lady approached and she spoke first. "My Lord Governor, I have done what you have asked - I have found a replacement to administer the small hospital and food store.
   He is a man of good character and is respected amongst the people. He has my full confidence and indeed my gratitude. I know that he will administer his duties kindly and fairly."

To this news the governor wasn't at all surprised, and did not feel the need to ask for any more information or proof, for he trusted her word.

He gave a small bow and said "Lady, you are truly remarkable. You have shown great kindness to the poor people that have made their home along this Great Wall; you have shown great determination in seeking what you desire from me and for this I congratulate you. I have here…" he took the Imperial document out from inside his woolly cloak "a document that gives you the complete ownership of the mountain you requested as a reward for all you have done for the people. I have this morning sent a messenger to the great eternal city of Rome to inform the Blessed

Emperor of my actions. I feel confident that he will agree with my decision."

Quintus Antistius wasn't as confident as he sounded but all he could do was hope that the Emperor agreed with him.

The lady smiled broadly and, taking the document, she said "Lord Governor, you have shown me great kindness this day. I am not surprised at all by your generosity for your name is one of greatness amongst the poor people. They know that you do the best you can for them as Imperial governor. I will leave you now. I do not think we will meet again, for this very morning I intend to travel south to the mountain you have so generously gifted to me but know this Lord Governor what you have done this day will have far reaching consequences and in time will play its part in protecting this province from a great enemy."

The governor did not understand what she meant by this but decided for some reason or other not to question it. Also why he did not ask her why she wanted to take ownership of a mountain in the middle of nowhere we will never know.

The lady again smiled, made a small curtsy, turned and walked towards the gate. She was almost through it when he called after her "Lady you have not told me your name or where you come from!" She turned and smiled and said "No, I have not" and for some reason this answer again came to no surprise to him. Deep inside he knew that was the answer he was going to get. He laughed and walked towards her, saying "Lady if you will not tell me your name I will ask only this of you, take this ring and remember me."

He took from his little finger a ring made of silver with an unusual white stone embedded in it. He handed it to her. The lady smiled and said of course she would remember him and said "You are a good man and your wife is a blessed lady to have such a husband." He looked at her with sadness in his eyes and said "My wife is indeed a fine lady but is childless. We would love to become parents but it's unlikely it will ever happen now." The lady smiled again and said "My dear man, worry not for your wife will have a child one day, I am sure of it." The governor laughed. "Do you really believe that?" "Do you?" said the lady. "Yes indeed, I would like to believe that" he said with a smile. "Then do so, for if you really believe something will happen then it will, and as much as this fine land that my heart belongs too will change in the years to come because of the great kindness you have shown me this day it will prevail."

   She smiled again, and taking the ring she put it on the second finger of her right hand. She thanked him again, turned, walked through the gates of the fort, turned left and was out of sight.

She was of course right that she and the Imperial governor of Britannia never met again. For his part he never forgot that week in March, for hers she had a silver ring with a white stone to always remind her of what a solemn promise always means and the absolute importance of trusting your fellow human beings.

Two years passed and news reached her at the mountain were she had made her home that the governor's wife indeed did have a child, a healthy daughter and they gave her the native Celtic name of Aoife.

In time she grew up and married and she too had children, one of which was a son. That little boy, whom she named Aled, grew up far from Hadrian's wall. He became a magnificent warrior and he forged a kingdom of his own in what we now call South Wales.

His descendants made Britannia their home and they didn't go back to Rome with the legions when they were recalled.

The governor didn't know it at the time of course but his little girl that he and his wife waited so long for would shape the future of these old islands in ways he could never have imagined.

Chapter 5
The Kingdom

It is now 250 years later, the Roman Empire has long fallen and there is chaos across the land.

Anglo-Saxon raiders from across the sea have devastated the land. There is war; bloody battles rage across most of the country; there is misery, starvation and death!

Although even in this carnage there are men and woman who will take a stand for freedom, peace and justice. There is such a man. He is brave and fearless; he is kind and chivalrous; he is a Prince; he rules over South Wales; his name and the names of his family members are lost to history; you won't find him on the list of Welsh princes, but he lived during the time when almost all of Britain was engulfed in war and battle!

His kingdom was the only place of relative peace on the entire island. His people were not war-like.

Instead they dedicated themselves to farming and horticulture. They lived off the land but they were cultured people. A lot of this was due in part to the professional army that protected South Wales Under their Commander Prince, the army was disciplined, loyal and of course well fed, and for a long time they held back the Anglo-Saxons who were jealous of this fruitful land. Soldiers patrolled the borders and great wooden forts were built along the boundaries to see off any one who threatened its tranquillity.

The Prince and his wife the Princess had four children - all girls - and each one was just as brave and fearless as their beloved father. They were loved by all in the kingdom.

His eldest daughter was the most inquisitive about the world around her and was interested in history and education.

His Second eldest daughter was gifted with the art of poetry and loved to write.

His third eldest daughter had a wonderful voice and could sing beautifully.

His last and youngest daughter was extremely brave. She would join the soldiers in their training exercises and was keen to learn the art of warfare. She was more like her father than her three sisters, and just like her father she also put peace, justice and fair play above all things. Their father was extremely proud of all four of them and loved his wife very much.

The kingdom came in to being some 250 years before. As we know the first Prince was the grandson of the Roman Governor Quintus Antistius. For 250 years the people lived in relative peace and were governed by his descendants- men and women who saw the importance not of war and conquest but of peace and prosperity.

The first Prince of South Wales was like his grandfather, and did not terrorise the people but encouraged them to live in peace, as did each Prince and Princess that came after him.

As much as there was peace and prosperity in South Wales, in the kingdoms to the west and to the north the people suffered greatly under unjust rulers. To the north a tyrannical queen ruled over her oppressed people. She lived in luxury and opulence but her people were close to starving. They lived in fear of this greedy queen who terrorised the land with an army of cutthroats and robbers!

To the west was a kingdom of Warriors. The people of that kingdom didn't care about learning, education or the arts. They didn't care about farming or peace. Just like their King all they cared about was war, both women and men alike. Indeed from a very young age even the children were taught how to use a sword. The kingdom was strong but without laws and infrastructure.

Beyond, much of the Island of Britain was ruled over and controlled by the Anglo-Saxons. There were several of these kingdoms and most of them were in a state of war with the other. Allegiances changed, sometimes on a daily basis, and no one could trust their neighbour.

The Anglo-Saxons who were jealous of South Wales, sent the occasional raiding party, though they could not break through the strong defences and most of the time they were too busy fighting with each other to pose any real threat.

As for the kingdom to the north, the tyrannical queen did not care about gaining more territory. All she cared about was pleasure and comfort, and had no interest in anywhere else except her own poor kingdom.

The western kingdom was ruled over by a man whose name we all know. He was strong, but conniving, unjust and untrustworthy. He ruled over a population of warriors, and his name was Uther Pendragon. He was jealous and envious of his neighbour in South Wales. Above all things he wanted the lands of South Wales for himself, but he knew that the Prince had a highly trained, well equipped professional army that was no match for his undisciplined rabble. They were greater in number but lacked the discipline and organisational skills to mount a full-blown invasion of his prosperous neighbour.

He was a bitter and cruel king, and he trusted no one. His wife had died in childbirth, leaving him with one son. This boy was named Arthur. Indeed the deeds of this boy will echo through the ages. His acts of courage will eclipse the actions of his treacherous father but his story is yet to come and plays no part in our tale for he was just a baby at this time in the distant and hazy past.

This part of the story starts here. It was mid October; the leaves on the trees were turning red, brown and gold; the summer harvest was well and truly over, and the days were growing shorter.

The Prince was in the castle with his wife and children a castle surrounded by a town that lay just two or three miles from where the ancient River Taff met the sea.

The town itself was a mixture of thatched houses with little chimney stacks on each one.

There were two or three inns, a small Church with a bell tower, and a town square with a busy market that sold all manner of goods such as meat, fish and vegetables. Some also sold such things as brooms, hats and wicker baskets. It was a hive of activity - the woman on the fish stores would cry out to let everybody know what was on offer and the man selling vegetables would do the same.

Anyone arriving in the town for the first time would be greeted by exquisitely carved oak gates under a great archway, for this town was completely surrounded by a great stone wall. The great west gate was the primary entrance for all who lived and worked in the town, and any one from the rest of the kingdom who would visit. It was guarded day and night by soldiers. The battlements were patrolled by archers and every man, woman and child inside and out of its walls felt safe and happy because of it.

A visitor to the town would pass through the carved gates and, up a sloping cobbled road, they would see the thatched houses. They would smell the smoke from the blacksmith on the right next to the Three Feathers Inn (how this public house got its name is indeed a wonderful story too but that is for another time). A little further on you would see the church and the bell tower that is overlooking the town square. There are children playing and people are chatting happily.

To the left of the square is the market, and to the right is the courthouse that stands alongside the cobbled road that runs through the centre of the town all the way up to the castle. If you were to walk up towards the castle you would (in the summer) see hanging baskets full of flowers and then suddenly you would hear the sound of running water, for outside the palace gates there is an ancient stone fountain.

A little further and you would come face-to-face with the tall imposing entrance to the castle. If you were to knock you would be invited in by a castle official.

Above the doors are the words in old Welsh.

Caru'r Gwlad,
Amddiffyn y bobolthis

It is the Prince's personal motto and in English reads:

Love The Land
Protect The People

The words are carved onto two separate oblong stones lying flat one on top of the other and they act as the lintel of the Castle doorway. This motto was that of the Prince's father, his father, and his father before him. For each Prince and Princess of South Wales were men and women of honour that indeed truly loved the land of South Wales and always honoured their duty of protecting the people.

Beyond the great doors there was a fine courtyard and in the middle was a statue of a dragon. It had been put there on the orders of another ruler of South Wales a very long time ago.

Outside the walls of the town for miles and miles around there were farms and villages. The thousands of people who lived here were happy and prosperous, they loved and respected their Prince and he loved and respected them in return for he was no tyrant.

Chapter 6
The Lady

It was around 1 o'clock in the afternoon and a plump woman came running in to the great hall where the Prince and Princess were just finishing their mid-day meal.

She was in a frenzy! "Begging your pardon Your Royal Highnesses but I have grave news!" To this they both stood up in astonishment! The woman they both recognised as the head cook from the castle kitchen! "What is it?" asked the Princess. The cook, realising suddenly where she was and who she was talking to, gave a somewhat rushed and wobbly curtsy and said "Ohhhh Your Royal Highness, my husband has just returned from seeing his Mam and he is in a terrible state! This morning on the road home he saw a.."

The cook stopped and looked suddenly embarrassed because this was the first time she had relayed her husband's terrifying story out loud but suddenly it sounded rather far-fetched not to mention rather stupid. The Prince then spoke in a calm voice and with a smile said, "Please calm down and continue. What was it that your good husband saw this morning?" The cook attempted another curtsy and said, "Begging your pardon your Royal Highness, my husband said that on his way home he saw a dragon!!"

To this the Princess laughed and said, "I'm sorry to jest but this cannot be true! The stories of dragons are but for children! There is no such thing. Yes the stories of such beasts used to be believed by all the people but that was long, long ago." The Prince however did not laugh, but looked at the cook and said "Where is your good husband now?" The cook explained that she had put him to bed because he was in shock at what he had seen! The Prince nodded and agreed that that was the best course of action. Before dismissing the cook he told her to take the rest of the day off and to bring her husband to see him tomorrow at 10 o'clock in the morning where he would hear his story for himself.

That evening, as the Prince got in to bed, the Princess began to question him, asking if he actually believed the story they had been told by the cook at luncheon that afternoon. The Prince told her that the cook and her husband were good and honest townspeople and tomorrow he would hear what the man had to say and decide for himself.

The news of a dragon in his kingdom was most unsettling for the Prince. As much as he had never seen a dragon, he like all the people had heard the stories of old that told of how great dragons would destroy entire towns and kingdoms. They were only stories, myths and legends but for him there was more to it, for on the day of his coronation some 22 years ago after the death of his beloved father, many people came from all over the Kingdom of South Wales to pay homage to their new prince. Among them was a lone woman who lived alone in a small house at the foot of a mountain some miles away, and during the celebrations this woman approached the new Prince when he was alone. "Greetings to you, my new Prince" she said and made a low curtsy. The handsome new prince smiled at her. She was very beautiful, her hair was tied back in a very complicated yet stylish fashion, her gown was of burnt orange, but unlike all the noble women of the kingdom who adorned themselves with all manner of jewellery, coronets, pendants hanging from gold chains, and diamond rings, this woman only had one ring. It was made of silver with a white stone and it was on the second finger of her right hand.

The Prince, looking at her in fascination, said in a somewhat lofty voice "You are welcome Ma'am. I trust you have all you need and you are enjoying the celebrations?" To this the woman's eyes that were as blue as the summer sky met the eyes of the Prince and she said, "Great Prince, I do indeed feel welcome, for it is a great day. The kingdom has a new Prince and the line of your father will indeed continue in you. I must leave soon and I have no gift for you." (It was customary for the people of the kingdom to bring gifts for the new Prince)

He smiled and told the woman there was no need and he would much prefer that his subjects used the money they would otherwise spend on gifts and presents for him on those in need. The woman nodded in agreement and said "Indeed, great Prince, I have no gift for you but I will say this: in the years to come, should any of your subjects report ever seeing a dragon in this kingdom, do not dismiss their story as fantasy and lies. Keep an open mind and on hearing such a thing come to me at my dwelling at the foot of the mountain that lays 8 or so miles north of here." Before the Prince could answer a voice behind him made him jump!

"My dear new grandson Prince! How handsome you look in your coronation regalia!" The Prince turned and standing there was his grandmother. Taking her hand and kissing it he said, "Dear grandmother let me introduce you to...." The Prince turned but the woman was gone, having left by the side door. Feeling confused, he followed his grandmother back into the ballroom where the celebrations continued long into the night.

The Prince never forgot the strange encounter on the day of his coronation, and now, 22 years later, it was indeed bothering him a great deal. He knew of course that dragons did not really exist! But he could not put out of his mind the advice this strange woman with beautiful blue eyes had given him. As his eyes closed and he drifted off to sleep, he quite decided that the following day he would indeed travel to the mountain and meet with this woman.

In the morning he informed the Princess that he would be travelling that day on an urgent secret mission. He would be grateful if she would speak to the husband of the cook to find out exactly what had happened the day before when he was travelling back to the castle from visiting his mother.

The Princess did not question this for she trusted her husband and she was more than used to him going off on secret missions at the moment's notice.

After breakfast the Prince and two of his most trusted and loyal lieutenants left the castle on horseback and headed north to the mountain.

His two men didn't question their prince as to where they were going or why. It was enough for them to be ordered to do so, not because he was "The Boss" and they simply did what they were told, or because they were afraid of what would happen if they did not obey him. No, they did what they did out of loyalty and respect for their prince. They, like all the soldiers in his army, had a great respect for him. He respected his men, for they were loyal, and each and every one of them would lay down their lives in his defence and the defence of South Wales.

As the three men travelled north, the people of the kingdom would stop what they were doing and cry out to him with joy, love and devotion to their great Prince.

The journey wasn't a long one. The Prince knew the mountain very well but until now had no reason to visit it because a lot of his time was dedicated to his family, his people and the safety of the kingdom. He had little time for recreational activities.

He knew only from other people that only one person lived at the foot of the mountain.

The three men did not feel as if they needed to stop and rest. They didn't stop until they saw the mountain and a little house nestled in its shadow. It was a truly beautiful scene. The leaves on the trees were turning red and gold and the whitewashed cottage stood out against the mountain.

As the three men approached, the front door opened and out walked a tall lady with blue eyes and long hair that fell down her back and she was holding a long staff. The three men got off their horses. All three gave a bow to the lady and to this she smiled and walked forward, gave a curtsy and said "My dear great Prince, you are indeed welcome! welcome to the three of you!" The Prince was looking at her with great astonishment, for this was indeed the same woman that came to see him 22 years ago. He had recognised her at once.

What astonished him even more was the fact that to his eyes this woman hadn't aged a day in that 22 years. In fact, the only difference was the colour of her dress and the style of her hair. Everything else was the same right down to the silver ring on her finger.

Before the Prince could say a word the lady spoke and said "Good men, inside my house you will find cheese, bread and ale set out on the kitchen table. Please accept my hospitality, for I wish to speak to your Prince alone." Both men looked at the Prince who smiled and told them to indeed go inside and eat.

They entered the little house, and into a small kitchen. There on the table was some freshly made bread and some delicious looking cheese and ale

The room was small but clean. There were bunches of herbs hanging in the window drying in the autumn sun. A small Welsh dresser stood against a wall with pretty plates set upon it. Smiling at each other the men sat at the table and began to eat.

Outside and when the front door closed, the lady asked the Prince to walk with her and as they walked the lady again spoke first. "Good Prince, again welcome to my home. You do not have to tell me why you are here, because I too have seen what brings you to me today. I have seen the beast. I saw it only yesterday and I knew that you would come. I also know that you have lots of questions including why, to your eyes, I haven't aged a day in 22 years. I know you want to ask me why I said what I said on your coronation day. Indeed, what made me give you that advice and warning? I will try and answer all your questions and advise you as best I can on how to deal with this threat not only to your kingdom but to all of Britain. Make no mistake, great Prince, there are dark and difficult days coming and you will need all your courage and strength, but take comfort because all of South Wales will stand with you, although you will have to make alliances with your neighbours."

To this last statement concerning his neighbours the Prince gave a great sigh because he knew that the kingdom to the north of South Wales was ruled over by a greedy and decadent queen with no interest in anything other than comfort and pleasure. He also knew that the kingdom to the west was ruled over by the most untrustworthy king west Wales has ever had. He knew that negotiations with those two people would be almost impossible.

The woman seemed to know what he was thinking and said "Nothing is impossible, great Prince, when people work together.

There is something else you must know: that a dragon cannot be defeated using any weapon that you possess. Nor can it be killed. Indeed, the best you can hope for is to capture and imprison it for as long as possible." The Prince stared into space for several minutes and then turned to look at the woman and said "Who are you and how do you know all of this? Indeed why haven't you aged a day in 22 years? Why did you come to me all those years ago and say the things you said?" The woman smiled and said "When next we meet I will answer all your questions. For now you must go home to your family.

Tell them everything, for you will need their courage and strength in the months to come but take heart, for the great dragon is not yet a danger to anyone. It has just awoken. I know this because someone told me of this a long, long time ago. I think that if it was at its full strength it would have indeed attacked your people by now and I know how devastating that would be! But soon it will be at its most deadly, and when that day comes you must act. You must be ready for it when it comes back in 40 days or so.

I however will come to you in six days time and we will talk more and prepare, but remember this, great Prince, a dragon is the most arrogant and vain creature that has ever lived. A dragon loves itself above all things and hates everyone and everything else."

When the Prince returned to his horse his two lieutenants were already mounted on their own horses. They thanked the woman for her hospitality. The Prince mounted his own horse, and the woman gave a smile and said, "We will meet again in six days time, great Prince." The three men said good-bye and then left for the castle.

Chapter 7
The Cook's Husband

Earlier that day in the castle the Princess was making arrangements to receive the husband of the cook who the day before made quite a claim - he told his wife that he saw nothing less than a dragon!!

This encounter supposedly took place when he was journeying home from visiting his widowed mother who lived some 25 miles away by the sea. His wife had burst in on the Prince and Princess in a state of hysteria. The Prince in his wisdom decided not to see him there and then to hear what he had to say, but to leave it until the man was rested after a good night's sleep. As we know, however, the Prince had left after breakfast to travel to the mountain and so it was left to his wife to see him in the great hall that morning. She had made arrangements for a member of the court to be present but only to write down the man's story in way of record so her husband, the Prince, could read it for himself on his return.

The Princess was in the great hall when there was a knock on the door; the courtier who was present to write down the man's story opened it. The cook's husband came in, stopped, bowed, and said, "Good morning Royal Highness. Thank you for seeing me." The Princess smiled and said, "Good morning to you too. Now, I trust you are rested and ready to tell me exactly what happened yesterday. My husband, the Prince, has been called away and has asked me to hear you."

The Princess, though sounding very official, had a kind and generous heart yet she found it incredibly difficult to believe that this man had indeed seen a dragon.

"Come, let us sit." She indicated two chairs near the window in the Great Hall. She sat first and then he. The courtier was sat at a desk.

"Now, good sir, I want you to tell me exactly what happened yesterday and what exactly you think you saw." The man, looking slightly nervous, began. He spoke for over 15 minutes, telling the Princess exactly what he had seen. The Princess for her part didn't ask any questions and made no attempt to interrupt him. From time to time the courtier looked up from his desk in disbelief at what he was hearing but he too did not say a word. The Princess had told him to write down every word and absolutely not to leave anything out.

By the time the man had finished both the Princess and the courtier were in a state of shock and disbelief.

The Princess stood up and smiled. She was indeed a gracious lady, and showed no shock or surprise at this man's story. She thanked him for coming and told him that the matter would be fully investigated. She also asked him not to tell anyone at all of what he had seen, lest he start a panic in the kingdom and to inform his wife to do the same. To this he agreed. She also told him that she had no doubt the Prince would have further questions for him in due course.

The man bowed out of the room.

The courtier, without any comment, handed the man's written story to the Princess and he too left the room. He was also told not to breathe a word to anyone.

By now the Prince was in sight of the town. The closer he got, the more concerned he became. How was he going to protect his beloved people from what was coming?

How indeed could he prepare his kingdom for something that could not be stopped or killed with any weapon? How could he ever consider an alliance with the neighbouring kingdoms? Until today he never once thought of dragons as real things, they were just stories.

He remembered being told of them as a child and he in turn would tell his four daughters stories of great dragons that would fly though the air and breath fire and destroy entire kingdoms! He tried to push those thoughts out of his mind as he rode though the carved gates of the town up the cobbled road to the castle.

Later that evening he was sitting alone in the private family quarters of the castle. He was waiting for his wife to arrive; he had a great deal to tell her of his visit to the lady at the mountain.

He had quite decided that he was not going to hide anything from her for he loved her and she deserved to know the truth. Ten minutes passed and the door opened. He stood up and greeted his wife with a kiss on the cheek. She looked tired and sat next to him near the fire.

"Dear husband, I have much to tell you." The Princess then told him all about how she had met with the cook's husband that morning and what he had told her. The Prince listened with a feeling of dread building inside him and he decided that he would hear what she had to say before he told her anything about his encounter with the woman at the mountain. The Princess handed him the scroll of paper she had brought with her. Part of him didn't want to read it - all of what he had been told that morning made the thought of reading it extremely difficult.

All the same it was very important that he find out exactly what was written on it. He smiled, took it from his wife and began to read. It was quite obvious that the courtier had indeed written down word for word exactly what the man had said, including the bad pronunciation as well as the irrelevancies.

"Well it was like this highness I had been to see me Mam cause she's been bad, her leg was up again and she didn't have much in so I took her some veg and bread I did some work for her and saw all was well before I started to walk 'ome and I got to half way and was about to sit to av' a rest at the bottom of an hill by the pool when I look across it and I saw it highness as big as this Castle! It was taking a drink and it didn't see me cause if it did I is sure I would be dead and my wife would be a widow now! I was full of fear 'cause I had never seen such a thing in all my life never in my dreams have I seen

such a beast! It was red as red as can be its wings so big that if it was to stand in the pool the wings would cross from end to end and a tale so long and full of ridges and scales with four big strong legs with great feet with claws the head was massive and it's eyes as black as night! It drunk for five minutes and took to the air with its great wings I was about a half a mile away but I could feel the wind from 'em!

Then I saw some sheep grazing on the far end of the pool the dragon did fly at them and opening its mouth three or four times but no fire came out and it then did fly away into the distance and out of sight."

The Prince put down the paper and just stared at his wife in complete disbelief. Indeed if he hadn't met with the lady at the mountain that day he would not have believed a word of it. Looking at his wife he was about to begin to tell her all of what he too had been told that day when there was a great banging at the door startling them both! "Come in" they both said at the same time!

The door opened and in to the room came a castle servant. He bowed to the Prince and Princess and said "Royal Highnesses, there is a man come to the castle wishing to have an audience with you both. He is from the Northern Kingdom. He informs me that he has a message for you both from his Queen and has strict orders that it is for Your Royal Highness' ears only." Looking at each other the Prince and Princess felt perplexed because it had been some years since there was any kind of communication from the Northern Queen. Indeed the last time was some five years ago and then it was only a threat regarding a border issue that the Prince didn't take very seriously, and suddenly out of the blue she has sent a Messenger.

"Then ask him to enter" said the Prince and to this the servant left the room. Moments later he returned with a scruffy little man wearing little more than rags. He looked very nervous and in need of a bath and a good meal. "You are welcome here, Sir" said the Princess looking at him with feelings of pity and curiosity. "Yes indeed, you are welcome" said the Prince. "We believe you have a message for us from your Queen."

The messenger looked sideways at the castle servant and at once the Princess realised what the problem was and asked the servant politely to leave the room, for she knew that the messenger was taking his orders seriously and would not speak to any one apart from her and the Prince. Closing the door behind him, the castle servant left the room. "Now good Sir, you may deliver your message" said the Prince. The man reaching inside his pocket brought out a roll of paper with two red ribbons attached to the bottom. He unrolled it and began to read....

"In the name of her gracious Majesty, Queen Imperial of the Northern realm, the most Highest and Mighty Queen, Sovereign of the Most High,...."

The Prince and Princess looked at each other and rolled their eyes. They both knew how conceited and proud this queen was, so it came to no surprise to either of them that she would adopt a title such as this. However neither of them made any attempt to interrupt as the messenger continued to read...

"We have, in our great wisdom and kindness, decided to honour you both with our presence. We know, of course, that this will fill you both with joy and happiness to have such a distinguished guest visit your small kingdom. We know, of course, that our presence will bring happiness to all your people and it will be a day of celebration and rejoicing across your small poor little kingdom. We know it will be a day that you will indeed look forward to.

We have decided to visit you at your dwelling three days from now and this will give you adequate time to prepare for my illustrious arrival, and celebrations can now be planned et cetera et cetera.

I do not wish to discuss the reason for my visit now, for this humble messenger would not be capable of understanding or reading the long words that I would have to use.

You may now prepare for my visit. Signed The Most Highest and Gracious Queen of the Northern Kingdom."

The Prince, hearing all of this, had to hold back a smile- never in his life had he heard such conceited nonsense! Although he understood how ridiculous this queen really was, he did not show it to her messenger, who indeed looked incredibly embarrassed after reading such lofty and conceited rubbish.

The Princess then said to the messenger, who was standing there looking straight-ahead, "Good sir, thank you indeed for delivering this message from your queen. We would like you to accept our hospitality, and we would like you to spend the night at the castle. Please go to the kitchens, eat your fill and have a good night's rest before you return to your kingdom." The Prince, who was nodding in agreement, then said "Yes, on your return tomorrow you may inform your queen that she is indeed welcome here three days from now." The messenger, smiling slightly at the prospect of eating his fill, bowed out of the room with words of thanks, for this man came from a land where even looking at his queen's face could put him in jail or worse.

A land where lack of food was a way of life, where the laws were made not for the good of all people but for the few and the rich.

This messenger did not have the freedoms that the people of South Wales enjoyed.

He was not free to speak his mind or to do as he wished.

The laws of his land were very harsh and the smallest of crimes could result in death. His life was one of endless work and fear, fear for his wellbeing and that of his family and friends.

For his queen was without love or mercy, and would think nothing of taking from those who have very little to give, and so this messenger made the best of the time he spent in South Wales and did indeed eat his fill and had a good night's sleep.

Chapter 8
A Call to War

The Prince knew there were difficult days to come not only for him and his family but for all his people and the entire kingdom.

The lady at the mountain had advised the Prince to tell his wife and his children everything, and he did take her advice. The following morning he sat down with his wife and four daughters and told them absolutely everything. He explained how the lady at the mountain had come to visit him on the day of his coronation and the warning she gave him; he told them about how he had visited her; he told them everything she had said and the encounter their mother had had with the cook's husband.

All four of them were indeed astonished, not to say terrified by all of this but without exception they assured their father that they would be at his side, and face whatever came and at that moment their father could not have been more proud of them.

As the days passed the Prince became more anxious.

He set in motion a plan that had been in place since he became Prince in his own right. It was a plan to deal with any kind of threat to his kingdom.

He called together all his most senior advisors from across the kingdom. His generals, magistrates, town officials et cetera were called to the castle to meet and discuss what could be a devastating time for his people and kingdom.

Also the Princess was organising the visit of the queen from the Northern Realm. Both tasks required a great amount of organising but both agreed that they would coordinate with each other, for the officials of the kingdom would indeed be summoned for a state visit anyway, and it would be a very good reason to prepare the kingdom for any eventuality.

The Prince did not trust the Northern Queen for he knew that her intention to visit must have something to do with the sighting of the dragon, and he also knew that she would be requesting his help in dealing with a grave threat not only to his kingdom but to hers as well.

Over the next two days all the officials began to arrive. The people of the kingdom were told their arrival was because of the visit of the Northern Queen. The Prince did not see any need to worry his subjects until it was absolutely necessary. The city was made ready and the people were in some ways looking forward to the queen's arrival, for many of them had only heard rumours about her. They knew of course that she was incredibly wealthy, but did not care very much about her people. She taxed them heavily and only cared about her own pleasure and comfort, but nevertheless the people of South Wales would welcome her in the same way as they would welcome any dignitary.

The town that surrounded the castle was made ready. Flags and bunting of white and green, the colours of the Royal house of South Wales, could be seen everywhere as well as red flags and bunting that represented the Royal house of the Northern Realm.

It was a cold but sunny morning. The Prince, Princess and their four daughters were dressed in their fine state robes. The Prince had put on his crown, as did the Princess. The four daughters were wearing beautiful tiaras and pinned to their gowns were their personal emblems and coats of arms, painted beautifully on discs made of solid silver. The eldest had a quill to represent her love of writing with a small crown above it. The second had a book to represent her love and dedication to poetry, again with a small crown. The third daughter had a musical note to represent her love for composing and singing, and like her two sisters had a small picture of a crown just above to represent her status. The fourth daughter had two crossed swords and a white dove- this was to represent her dedication to the defence of the realm and her love of peace again with the crown above it.

It was the day before the Northern Queen was due to arrive. The Prince had decided to hold a meeting with his dignitaries before the Northern Queen arrived and to tell them all of the dragon, and hopefully together they could formulate a plan, and he wanted to hear their advice.

He also wanted to set in motion the contingency plans for the safety of each and every citizen of South Wales and he would be issuing the appropriate orders for things like emergency food supplies and the activation of all reserve soldiers that would happen after the Northern Queen had left.

The doors opened and in a clear and incredibly loud voice came the words, "The General of his Royal

Highnesses' Army!" The announcement came from a man standing by the door. He would be announcing every man and woman that would enter. Next was, "His Excellency the Mayor of Ogmore," and then came, "Matron and Chief Healer of South Wales," and next came, "His Excellency Lord Glamorgan," and by the time he had finished there were over 30 people standing in rows before their beloved Prince and his family. Indeed they were the most important people in the land. They were all in one way or another entrusted with the safety and welfare of the people and the Prince was about to address them on a subject that he knew would cause a great deal of worry and distress. He was certain that each man and woman in that room would like him have heard the stories about dragons, but would have never thought of them as anything other than childish stories.

Stepping forward, and after greeting them all he began, and just like with his four daughters he did not leave anything out. He told them every detail for he trusted each and every one of them. He also knew that each one would do their duty in the defence of the realm.

As he spoke the dignitaries began to gasp and by the time he was finished each and every one of them wanted to speak first. The Prince held up his hands for silence and said, "My good people, our kingdom is about to face its greatest threat and I now look to you for your advice and counsel. Please, I can only hear you if you speak one at a time." Pointing at a woman standing in the second row he said, "Matron, you served my father and his father before him. You assisted my mother to give birth to me, you assisted my wife to give birth to our four daughters, and now I must ask you again not only to serve me, but the entire Kingdom. Please give me your counsel."

She was an old woman with grey hair and a hard face, but her eyes were bright and sharp. Her dress was long and black, and covered all of her body, with a high collar. She stepped forward and made a courtesy and said, "My sovereign, indeed our home is threatened. I have lived here for 89 years and in that time I have seen a great many things, good and bad but now it will be my honour to serve you and this glorious kingdom. Indeed it will probably be the last time I will do so. I suggest that emergency hospitals are set up in each town and village.

I would like to see each and every citizen with any kind of medical knowledge to report here to the castle as soon as possible for supplies and instruction. I would also recommend that we convert the castle ballroom in to a hospital for wounded soldiers should it be needed, and I will administer to that myself."

The Prince smiled and said, "Matron, you are indeed a great woman. All you have suggested will be put into motion immediately. Use all the resources that you see fit." The old matron again curtsied and stepped back in line.

The next to speak was a tall man. He was a man of business and he had an understanding of distribution of goods, food and supplies. He assured the Prince that food supplies and clean water, as well as the medical supplies that the matron would need, would be made available to all that needed it. Supply lines would be planned and secured. Again the Prince told him that it would all be done as he has said.

In the front row stood the general and he was the highest ranking soldier in the kingdom under his commander Prince. He was responsible for the day to day running of the army. He oversaw the defence of the borders. He was brave and courageous, and was fiercely loyal to the Prince and the kingdom. When he was a young man he served as a foot soldier and climbed the military ladder to become a general. He was battle hardened, his face was scared and two of his fingers were missing. The entire army, not to mention the entire kingdom, had a great deal of respect for him for he had never lost a battle in 50 years of devoted service.

For as much as the General was feared in battle he was a kind and true gentlemen and he, like the Prince, knew of the threat that was coming. He spoke for some time of the army and how it was ready for anything. He asked the Prince if all reserve soldiers could be called up and all the blacksmiths in the kingdom told to make weapons. The Prince agreed to all of this.

Each man and woman spoke and gave advice to their Prince and each and every one of them re-pledged their loyalty.

As the officials of the kingdom made their leave, each bowing and curtsying as they left the room, the Prince was smiling at each of them, but behind his smile was a sense of fear. He would not let his kingdom fall and if it did he would never let it be forgotten!

That afternoon he made a visit to the one lady he knew would make sure that the history of his people and his kingdom was kept safe. She was the court librarian, and she knew the history of the kingdom better than anyone. He knew that she would keep a full record of everything that may happen in the coming days. She was a very clever woman and the Prince asked her to fully document the visit of the Northern Queen.

Within the Great Library there were books and manuscripts that dated back to the founding of the kingdom some 250 years ago.

The Prince asked the librarian if he could look at any documentation there maybe regarding dragons. To this the librarian seemed surprised, but did not comment, and directed the Prince to the section of the library that contained myths and legends. There were a great deal of old dusty books, scrolls and manuscripts piled one on top of the other on bookshelves that reached the ceiling. There were books on ancient mythology and old obscure legends.

The Prince allowed his eyes to travel upwards. He saw books with such titles as "***Legends of Albion***" and '***Ghosts of Glamorgan.***'

Suddenly his eyes became fixed on a book just above his head, with faded red writing along its spine read the words "**The Dragons of the World**." At first he hesitated but with little trouble he managed to take down the book. It was very old and its pages were brittle and yellowing with time.

The hard cover was plain with no writing upon it and so sitting at a small desk, the Prince began to read. It wasn't an easy task for the writing was in some parts faded away altogether. It was in an old primitive form of Welsh, and the Prince had some trouble understanding it.

It was a book of stories and legends regarding dragons from places with strange names and back when the world was a very, very different place. Some he had heard before, but others such as a story about how a dragon once destroyed a city where the people had lived forever and could not be killed by anyone or anything other than a dragon.

He spent hours reading, but there was no clue anywhere in the book on how to kill a dragon. He never really expected to find anything because the Lady of the Mountain had already told him that it was impossible to slay a dragon.

The other thing that he found strange was that there was no author's name in the book, nor did the librarian have any idea indeed who wrote it or where it came from. She told him that it had been in the library for as long as she had been in charge. He told her to keep the book safe and that he would return and read it again soon.

Chapter 9
The Northern Queen

He made up his mind that the best thing to do was to get the visit of the Northern Queen out of the way and then wait for the woman at the mountain to come to him. The woman at the mountain had made it clear that he would need to make alliances with his neighbours, and that was exactly what he planned to do the following day when at last he would meet the Queen of the North. He knew of her reputation of arrogance, but he had a secret weapon and that was his wife and he would let her lead for there was no one in the world he trusted more and he knew that his beloved wife could handle this decadent queen.

The morning came and it felt as if the entire kingdom had come out to catch a glimpse of a queen they had heard so much about but until today never got the chance to see. Hundreds of people had come to witness this historical event, for no king or queen from North Wales had ever made such a visit until today.

By tradition, the Queen was due to arrive at midday. At 11:30 that morning the Prince, the Princess and their four daughters again dressed in robes and crowns were preparing to make their way out into the Great Courtyard to receive their royal guest from the North when suddenly the palace trumpeters could be heard! Looking at each other, the Prince and Princess at the same time said, "She is 30 minutes early!" Laughing the Prince said, "We should have foreseen this happening! We should have known she would have tried to catch us unprepared!" and he could not have been more right!

And so hurrying to the doors of the castle the royal family walked down the steps and into the courtyard, just in time to witness something quite extraordinary. First they could hear a great deal of cheering from the people outside, and then six handsome white horses came through the archway, pulling behind them the most elaborate carriage anyone had ever seen. It was made of silver and gold. On the top was a great oversized crown studied with real jewels. The wheels too were covered in diamonds and other precious stones. The entire thing was gleaming in the sunlight but it looked so out of place and over the top that it could not be taken seriously.

Then there came the rest of the entourage. Five wagons packed with all manner of things including what looked like an enormous chair or indeed throne. There were foot men, then ladies in waiting, soldiers, men with fine hunting dogs, women with falcons and all manner of other courtiers and servants numbering over fifty people.

The carriage stopped in front of the royal family and the entourage lined up behind it. The coachman jumped down and hurried to open the carriage door. Out of the carriage came two ladies in waiting who stood either side of the little steps leading up to the open door. Then there came the most extraordinary sight imaginable.

The Queen of North Wales wasn't anything the Royal family had expected. She was a short, stout woman. Her face had so much white make up upon it that one could be forgiven for thinking that she had fallen headfirst into a barrel of flour.

Her eyebrows looked as if they had been painted on with ink. Her lips were a bright red, her eyes looked cold and fierce, and her ears were sagging with the weight of great diamante earrings.

She was wearing a ludicrous blonde wig with a great diamond encrusted crown perched on top of it, and indeed her gown for a moment looked as if it was made entirely of diamonds and pearls, rubies and sapphires. The Prince was surprised she could even walk with the amount of precious stones that adorned her. She was carrying a staff of gold and standing on the red carpet she appeared to be waiting impatiently for her official welcome to the kingdom.

The state herald who was standing next to the Royal family began to read the state welcome....

"In the name of his Royal Highness, the Prince and sovereign of South Wales, and on behalf of all the people of South Wales, we today welcome our Royal guest her Majesty the Queen of North Wales! May she always be prosperous and enjoy a long and healthy life!"

There was silence and in a deep and somewhat irritated voice, the Northern Queen said "Is that it? Is that to be my welcome? I am a great Queen who has travelled far to this funny little kingdom to bring you news of great importance. That is the welcome you have prepared for me?!"

The Prince, who was not at all surprised by this response chose to completely ignore what she had said, stepped forward as his wife the Princess and his four daughters, in accordance with protocol, curtsied to the ungrateful Queen. Holding out his hand he welcomed her. She took his hand briefly and shook it. He then formally introduced her to his wife and daughters. She eyed each one of them with suspicion and made derogatory comments about their clothing and jewellery (all of which were ignored) and as she did so she smiled a smile that made them all feel uncomfortable!

The Prince then invited her into the castle where, again in accordance with tradition, the Princess took over. She showed the queen to a suite of rooms that were kept for important visitors. They were both spacious and decorated beautifully with tapestries and paintings, but not surprisingly the queen managed to find fault with almost everything about her accommodation. "I don't like the view from my window" and "I don't like the tapestries" and "The bed is too small" (although she was only just over 5 foot tall). The Princess explained that accommodation would be found for her rather large entourage but the queen didn't appear to even hear what she had said and it was well known that the Queen didn't care about her people.

    Preparations were well underway for the state banquet that evening. All the officials of the kingdom would be in attendance. The Prince still didn't really know for certain why the Northern Queen had decided to visit but he intended to find out and talk with her about a possible alliance, which of course would mean having to tell her about the dragon.

He sent word to her rooms to inform her that he would be calling on her to 'hold talks' and then at 3 o'clock he was shown in to her chamber.

The Queen was sitting on what could only be described as a throne. Her appearance was almost comical: she was surrounded by servants and jesters, the blonde fright wig had been replaced with a short black one and there was no crown but she still looked like a pantomime dame.

Greeting her, the Prince asked if they could talk privately. Agreeing somewhat reluctantly, the Queen clapped her hands and commanded everyone to leave the room at once. When they were alone she did not invite the Prince to sit down but simply stared at him, and then without any warning she said in a venomous whisper, "I suppose you know all about the dragon that has been seen flying over Wales?" The Prince didn't see any reason to lie and nodded; he told the Queen that one of his people had seen it just days before and that he planned to do all he could to protect his people. He did not feel it necessary at that point to mention the Lady of the Mountain or about the fact that he intended to open up negotiations for a possible alliance with the Western Realm.

The Queen too showed no surprise at the fact her host knew of the dragon. Eyeing him intensely she said, "Well, what are you going to do about it? You have a massive army don't you? You must kill it!"

The Prince wasn't at all surprised at this statement either. He realised very quickly that she had come to him for help for he was a clever man and knew what she wanted.

They talked for some hours. She, like him, had heard the stories of old. They told of a great winged beast that could bring down kingdoms and destroy everything it saw.

The Queen up until this point was letting the Prince do most of the talking. The sun had set and suddenly the Queen said "Do you know where it came from?" Her voice for the first time sounded almost worried, for up until now all she did was make demands of the Prince telling him that it was up to him to save them all.

The Prince had no idea where the dragon came from, nor did he much care. His only concern was to protect his people from it. He told the Queen, who looked surprised and said, "Surely you know that it came from across the sea? It came from the land of the Danes. My spies tell me that it was released by men in the pay of Uther Pendragon!!"

The Prince, who by now had found himself his own chair, did not react to this news but the Queen seemed to be enjoying herself. She was a mean and pompous woman and took great pleasure in other people's worries and misfortunes. She knew of course that the Prince had no idea that Uther Pendragon had anything to do with it, and her entire visit was leading up to telling him this news.

He did his upmost not to show her his surprise at this news, although she could not or would not tell him anymore about it. He knew that this news would change things dramatically.

The Queen spent the next half an hour drumming it into the Prince that he needed to act and that her army, although far superior to his, was far too busy to capture and potentially kill the dragon.

The Prince of course knew that this was a lot of rubbish. He knew because he too had spies and they told him that North Wales didn't really have an army, just a large group of thugs who terrorise the people on behalf of their tyrannical queen.

It was also evident that the Queen had no idea that the dragon could not be killed by any weapon either of them possessed. The Prince decided not to share this piece of information with her at this point, preferring to keep that particular point to himself for the time being. He did however raise the question of a possible military alliance but the queen did seem to want to consider it and simply gave him a flat no!

Later that evening the state banquet was well under way. The Great Hall of the Castle was filled with all the officials of the kingdom. Sitting at the top of the table was the Prince and the Queen.

There were toasts and speeches and when the Queen spoke it wasn't to thank her hosts or to talk fondly about her visit but to tell everyone who was there how grateful they should be for her visit. She did of course hint at the fact that she had given the Prince some grave news but stopped short at saying what it was.

The next day was more or less the same. The Princess had arranged a tour of the town that should have taken some hours but didn't last more than 45 minutes, for the Queen deliberately rushed through it and didn't show any interest saying "Your people seem to have far too much leisure time! In my realm my people work hard and never have time to sit about."

The Princess did not comment and as they returned to the castle, the Queen turned to her and said "I am leaving tomorrow, please see to the necessary arrangements." The Princess was of course very surprised at this because according to tradition a royal visit would last five days. However the Princess didn't think anyone including herself would be sorry to see this rude decadent queen leave.

The royal family again dressed in their finest and standing in the courtyard of the castle were awaiting the Queen of the North to leave. She kept them waiting (probably on purpose) over 40 minutes before she made an appearance. All her belongings had been packed away and her entourage were waiting all lined up behind the diamond encrusted carriage.

The court trumpeters began to play, and the short little Queen came out of the great doors and walked down the steps, again in a blonde wig with a great crown set upon it. Walking past the royal family and without a word, she got into her carriage but just before she gave the order to the coachman to leave she beckoned the Prince to the carriage window and whispered something to him. The Prince nodded and stepped back. Smiling a nasty smile the Queen thumped the roof of the carriage with her golden staff and looking straight ahead she and her entire entourage left the courtyard through the stone arch and out of sight.

The entire court was quite honestly glad to see the back of her! Had there ever before been such an awkward guest in the castle? The Prince was also pleased at her departure but it left him with some questions: Did Uther Pendragon really have anything to do with the dragon? If so why and where was the Dragon released from exactly? He didn't know any of the answers and his only hope was the Lady of the Mountain. Maybe she could answer his questions.

That evening when the Prince and Princess were quite alone, they talked about the Queen's visit and the Prince told his wife all the Queen had said during their private conversation, all about how Uther Pendragon had somehow paid someone to release the dragon and it came from far across the sea. Up until now his wife, like him, never really gave much thought to where the dragon came from. They talked for some time. Neither of them could really come up with any answers.

The Princess then asked her husband what the Queen had said to him just before she left. Smiling the Prince answered, "She told me that it was only I that could save us all! But I don't know how I am going to do that my dear. This problem isn't going to go away and we have very difficult times to come, but my dear it has been a very long day and I really do think it is now time that we get some sleep."

Chapter 10
The lady and her Story

It was a cold morning, and the Prince was standing at a small window looking out over the town and countryside beyond. This land was part of him, and he loved it like a fifth child. He knew that whatever came he must face it with courage and bravery. Today was the sixth day and at some point that day the Lady from the Mountain was due to visit him. He did not know what time the lady would arrive or what she was going to say, but he knew that she would come.

As he looked across the land he loved he saw it. His eyes were fixed upon it and it was as if the town, the country side, the sky and the land had died away and all that was left was what the Prince could see. He could not move, his body was on fire, he knew what he was looking at but he could not believe it. What he was looking at was a great mass flying across the sky. It was red as red as can be; its wings were a colossal size; its tail was long and full of ridges and scales and had four big strong legs with great feet with claws; the head was massive and it's eyes as black as night! The dragon was flying low across the sky. It was about a mile away but for a split second the Prince felt as though it was looking at him and it was as if their eyes met, but within less than 30 seconds it was gone- it seemed to have flown out of site.

The Prince still could not move. He had seen it, and for the first time in his heart he knew it was real.

Up until now a part of him had hoped that it had all been a trick or a joke but no, it was all true and dragons were not just stories but very real.

Suddenly the Prince was pulled out of his trance like state. His eyes again saw the town and land. He could hear a great deal of shouting from the town, and he knew at once that he had not been the only one to see the dragon. The townspeople must have seen it too. He also knew that the time had come to tell his people everything, and that was what he did, and so by the end of that day each man, woman and child in the town knew that a dragon had been seen over the kingdom.

He had sent out messengers not only to the town but to every part of his kingdom. It would take some days for his message to reach all his people but it was the best he could do. The messengers also asked each man aged 20-45 years old to come to the town for military service.

It was coming up to midnight and the Prince, who had not seen his family all day, at last sat with them to eat in the small informal private part of the castle. His wife had spent the day overseeing the castle ballroom being made in to a hospital as recommended by the Matron. His four daughters too had been busy: they helped organise the men who were coming from the town to answer the call of their beloved Prince. Accommodation had to be found for them. They needed to be fed too. The four young Princesses did all they could to find them somewhere to sleep.

As the family sat and talked over their late dinner there came a knock at the door, and in came a housemaid.

She told the Prince that a strange woman had come to the castle and she asked to speak with him and that she was expected. The Prince knew of course who the maid was talking about and asked that she be shown in at once. The maid left the room. Within minutes there was again a knock at the door. In came the maid with a tall woman with blue eyes. Her hair was tied back. She smiled at the Prince and his family. The Prince asked the housemaid to leave the room and close the door and then, standing up, he introduced the lady to his family. The lady curtsied to all five of them. The Prince then asked her to sit down at the table.

The Princess gave the lady a glass of wine. No one spoke for some time until at last the Prince said "Thank you lady for keeping to your word and coming here this day. As you must know, the great beast has now been seen by a great deal of my people I have put into motion emergency plans to defend my kingdom and her people from this dragon." He went on to tell the lady all that had happened. He told her of the meeting he had held with the officials of the kingdom, the visit of the northern Queen and what she had told him, he told the lady how that very morning he too had seen the dragon flying across the land.

The lady did not speak but just smiled and nodded as the Prince spoke. She sipped her wine and then said "My Prince, I think the time has come for me to tell you a story."

Smiling at the five of them she said "I know that you are doing all you can to defend this land and its good people, but as I told you before there is no weapon in the world that can harm or kill it. There is only one thing you can do and that is to try and catch it and make it sleep." To this the Prince and his family did not know what to say. The lady knew what they were thinking and said "My good people, I ask you now to hear what I have to say. I know you may think I am mad but I ask each and every one of you to trust me and hear what I have to say."

The Prince, his wife and their four children all then made themselves comfortable at the table and, smiling, the lady began her story.

"My story begins just like anyone else's on the day of my birth. I cannot tell you the day or the month because when I was born time meant something quite different to what it means now, but it was a time before the great ice sheets covered the land. It was a beautiful land and my people were the first of what you would call humans to inhabit this continent. They came here from the south to Europe when there was room on earth for all of us. My people were good and hardworking. They were artists and philosophers, and although they only numbered around 1500 people, our civilisation was a strong one. We were cut off from all the other peoples in this world.

Violence and war were alien to us, as was cruelty and suffering. We knew nothing of pain or want, and although occasionally someone would have an accident, we knew nothing of illness or disease.

Indeed we built a civilisation in one of the most remote areas on this planet. My people lived for hundreds and hundreds of years. Death simply did not exist for us. I cannot tell you why that was so, but I can tell you why only I and one other of my kind is left. I remember it as clearly as yesterday and it was a day that changed my life forever.

I woke up like I did each morning. My family lived in a small house that had been there for centuries and I loved it so. Just like every day I greeted my mother and father at the first meal, and just as we were about to eat there was a terrible sound of screaming. We ran outside and what I saw was terrifying! It was a great beast of the like I had never seen before! I was used to the wild animals like mastodons and woolly rhinoceroses but this was a beast of titanic proportions. Its wings were huge, and its body was five times the size of a woolly mammoth with a tail to match! It was flying over my settlement and breathing great plumes of fire. People were being burnt alive and dying! I could not move as I was frozen with fear! Some men were throwing spears at it but they simply bounced off.

    Without thinking my father run out to join the men who were trying to subdue the beast, but he, along with them, was killed in a great plume of fire!

    Terrified, my mother and I ran into the house but it was no good for the beast saw us run and spat fire in the direction of the house!

My mother pulled open a trap door in the floor and pushed me in. It was her intention to join me in the small pit underneath the house that we kept for storing food, but it was too late and the deadly fire came in through the open front door of the house and as it did with my father, it killed my mother. I lay there on the floor surrounded by supplies for what seemed like a day. I could hear screaming and carnage outside.

I think I fainted, and when I woke there was deadly silence. I eventually got the courage to leave the store pit and when I went outside the sight that met me was one of complete devastation. Everything was completely destroyed, and each and every person in my home was dead. Everything I knew was gone, all of my people were dead and I was the only one left alive. I was alone.

The years passed and I became used to my solitude. The weather became colder with each passing year until finally ice started to cover the high ground. By then I had left my home and headed east.

A great deal of time passed before I saw anyone that resembled me, but they were different to the people I had known. They were violent and territorial, they did not like strangers.

They were suspicious of me so I never stayed in one place for too long, until one day I stumbled upon a small village. The people were kind and welcoming. It had been over a thousand years since I had met anyone who was willing to let me spend some time with them, and I welcomed the chance to maybe make friends.

They indeed welcomed me and it was there and from them I learnt so much.

I got to know and understand what it meant to be part of a community again.

They were a good and kind people, but they did not live for more than 40 or 50 years and I came to realise that they had absolutely no concept of immortality. However they had a deep and rich culture and I did absolutely nothing to change their beliefs around life and death, and because of this I knew I could not stay with these people for more than a few years, less they grow suspicious that I was incapable of ageing.

I made up my mind that the day was coming when I must leave, and for a very long time my heart had been telling me that I should travel north and across the sea to a land that the people of the village didn't really believe existed but, they called it Albion. According to their stories it was a land of mystery and untold wonder. I felt an overwhelming urge to visit this mysterious land and see it for myself and indeed find out if it truly did exist."

The Prince, who had been listening intently, looked up at the lady and said, "Only days ago when I visited the castle library did I read of a city whose people lived forever, until a dragon came and killed them all and destroyed the city. Are you one of those people and was that your home?"

The lady smiled at the Prince and said, "Yes, my Prince, and the book that is now in your library was written by the only other of my kind to survive that terrible day. I did not know until much later that there was another just like me."

The youngest of the Prince's daughters coughed gently and said, "Please lady, continue with your story." Smiling the lady continued.

"My days were filled with work and endless contentment. At night I would join the villagers in their great hall, and by the light of the fire they would tell stories of their ancestors. There was one re-occurring theme and each story they told mentioned what you would call a dragon!

"They knew of the dragon, although not one of them had actually ever seen one, or so I thought. I of course had, but I knew better then to mention it. One thing was for sure they viewed the dragon with fear.

"The stories were of how dragons once numbered tens of thousands and ruled the Earth. They came in all shapes and sizes but one day a great rock fell from the sky and hit a far away land. The force was so strong that it killed almost all of them. The ones that were left started to hunt and kill each other until only five or six remained"

"The chieftain of the village was a kind and wise man. He taught me a great many things, but he never once asked me where I came from, although I also had the feeling that he knew I wasn't quite the same as his people.

"We would walk and talk for hours until the day came when I finally decided that I must leave the village less the people notice that unlike them I simply did not age.

"The day before I was due to leave the chieftain asked me to his hut. I knew almost instinctively that his invitation wasn't just to say good bye.

"It was very cold but the sun was bright and there wasn't a cloud in the sky. I felt a great sadness but I knew that I had to leave.

"As I entered the chieftain's hut it took several seconds for my eyes to adjust to the dim light inside. The first thing I saw was the old man sitting on a simple wooden bench. He was very old but with a kind face and I had a great respect for him. He was nothing like the other tribal leaders I have met since my home was destroyed so many years ago. He wasn't war-like but fiercely defended his village against anyone who threatened it.

"As I walked forward I knew that there was something incredibly different about his hut today. I had been invited in many times but today was quite different, for everywhere I looked there were small statues and rough paintings, with models made of wood or grass packed in to this small hut! There were over 200 of them and each and every one was a variation of the same thing - they were all representations of dragons! My eyes moved from one to the other with a feeling of fascination and dread! I wanted to run from the hut but I could not move!

Before I could speak and ask him why he had such a collection he smiled and simply said, "How old are you woman?" This was the very last thing I expected him to say. For a moment I could not answer, I just stared at him in surprise and disbelief! He spoke again and invited me to sit next to him on his wooden bench and I did so, but all the time I could not take my eyes off his vast collection!

"After a few minutes I gathered my thoughts and pulled myself together, and I began to calm down. Looking directly at him I asked him why he had such a collection in his hut and why I hadn't seen it before. To this he simply smiled and again asked me how old I was. This of course wasn't the first time someone had asked me my age and I always give the same answer. When I was asked my age I always said I was 28 years old, and most people were satisfied with the answer I gave. In reality my true age by his calendar and understanding I was around 5000 years old, but I never revealed that to anyone because as far as I knew it was only my people who never died of illness or old-age. Since the dragon destroyed my home and my people I assumed that I was the only one left and I saw little good in telling anyone the truth, so I said I was 28 years old. The chieftain simply laughed, but did not press the issue and then at last he looked me straight in the eye and said, "You want to know why I have this collection of dragons? You want to know why I have chosen today of all days to show them to you?" To this I just nodded enthusiastically. He stood up and walked over to a small clay model, picked it up and said, "Lady I know that you are much older than you claim to be. In fact I think you are thousands of years old.

I think you came from a kingdom that is even today being consumed by the sea and your people, although long gone now, lived for an extremely long time.

The diseases that kill my people did not affect the people you once called kin, that much I know for certain."

"By now I had butterflies in my stomach, my mouth was dry and I could not understand how this man could possibly know all of this but I remained silent as he continued..."

"Lady I think you know of the dragon. I have watched you when my people speak of great winged beast that breathes fire! I have seen the look in your eyes and I have seen the fear!

Also, your eyes are the colour of the brightest summer sky and they are nothing like the eyes of my people and now I will tell you one last tale before you leave tomorrow"

"I did not know what to say to him. I knew of course that everyone in the village had brown eyes and mine were blue, but until then no one had ever mentioned it, As for my homeland being consumed by the sea he was right, for once my home was green and beautiful, but now it was just a collection of uninhabited Islands some miles across the sea to the north but I had not been there for some time.

"There was a brief silence and I told him that my eyes were the same colour as the tribe to which I belonged.
He looked at me in a way that seemed as if he could read my mind. He did not however mention my eye colour, my home land or indeed my age again. He simply said "Lady before you leave tomorrow I wish to tell you a story.
It's a true story that was told to me when I was a boy by a man I thought was going to kill me! I can remember it as if it were yesterday. I was around 14 years old and hunting in the Black Forest to the east. I was alone and I came to a clearing. There was only an hour or so of day light left and I needed to start a fire for the night. Then suddenly out of nowhere there was a great rush of wind from above. Looking up I saw a beast the size of nothing I have ever seen before. It was red in colour and truly massive. It's wings stretched out, it's tall longer than any serpent and a head the size of a mammoth! I was truly terrified but out of fear and fascination I could not move. The beast then landed in

the clearing. It did not notice me when I finally pulled myself together and jumped behind a tree. My heart was beating so fast I could feel it in my chest! The air around me was hot and I felt sick! The dragon did not see me as it began to lay down and sleep. I knew that this creature had never been seen by my people before but they knew of it and told stories about it. Up until now I just thought they were just stories, for I like everyone else had heard the stories of great winged beasts, but I also thought they were just childish tales invented by adults to frighten their children if they refused to behave. I never thought of them as real, but I was wrong!

"I was about to run home and tell the village all about it but just then I saw carved in each tree surrounding the clearing, images of dragons. There were over 100 of them, and I could not understand why but I did not care! All I wanted to do was run away. As I turned I was pushed to the ground by a hooded man carrying a wooden staff. He came upon me.

He was much stronger than I. He put his hand over my mouth and in my ear he whispered "silence" and I was terrified. He told me that he would kill me if I made a sound to disturb the dragon. He then went on in a whisper, still with his hand over my mouth that the great beast would only sleep if it knew that its image surrounded it and that was why the trees had the carvings I had noticed. He told me the dragon was capable of destroying entire tribes with fire and it had done so many times before. He told me to leave that place and never ever return! Dragging me from the floor he told me to always be prepared and always have the image of a dragon available to protect myself and my tribe. Taking hold of my arm, and through gritted teeth, he told me that if I ever saw the creature fly across my homeland it meant that it had just awoken. It meant that it was weak and could not breathe fire, but that would not last and it would return in 40 days and completely destroy everything because that is what it did best!

"He then told me to go home and never ever return to this place!

"'Without another word he disappeared into the trees but not before taking down his hood and looking me in the eye and said, "remember me boy." His eyes were as blue as yours, lady, and you are the only other I have ever seen with blue eyes.

"It took me five days to get back to this village and I decided not to tell anyone of what I had seen in the Black Forest but from that day to this I have made models, carved statues and drawn pictures of dragons and kept them hidden under the floor of my hut just in case that great beast ever appears in the skies above this village."

"The chieftain had a great deal of relief in his face. I think I was the first person he had ever told of what happened all those years ago. I did not speak but let him continue.

"I have no idea who that man was in the Black Forest that day, but since then I have heard rumours of a wise man who is thousands and thousands of years old who came from a land that has been almost taken by the sea, but they have always only ever been rumours. The years passed, and when my father died and I became chieftain of this village I saw that my people never ventured into the Black Forest. I fabricated a story that the Great Black Forest was haunted and did all that I could to discourage my people from ever going there and it has always worked."

"Smiling, he stood up and told me he had nothing more to say and he was not going to ask me any more questions about my age or where I came from, but taking my hands and looking me in the face he said 'Tomorrow you will leave this place and my people. We will never meet again, but please always remember us, and more importantly please always remember what I told you this day and should it ever be in your power do not let the great beast destroy another civilisation.'

"After he kissed me on both hands and wished me a happy life, I left the hut. As I left I knew, as he did, that we would not meet again. The rest of my day I spent with the friends I had made in the village. I would miss them, but for their sake I knew I had to leave. As the sun set I went back to my own dwelling to sleep for the last time in my own bed.

"I awoke before sunrise and before any of the villagers. I gathered together my one or two belongings, got on my horse and I left. There were tears in my eyes as I headed north out of the village. I didn't know what the day would bring but my plan was to head north and across the sea to the land the people called Albion.

Chapter 11
The Meeting of my Kin

"I didn't glimpse any one for weeks. I slept in the open air next to a small fire. The little food I had with me was quickly running out until I came to a small, rather primitive settlement near the sea coast. There were great wooden posts that completely surrounded the entire hamlet. I could just see the tops of huts over the high fence and one or two had smoke coming out of holes in the roof.

"The great wooden gates looked unwelcoming but because of need and the onset of hunger I knew I had little choice but to ask for help. I would offer to work for food and so, getting down from my horse, I approached the wooden gates. The closer I got I began to notice that the wooden gates were completely covered in carvings.

They were crude and not very well done, but into both doors were carved images of dragons! I felt apprehensive. Did the people who lived here know of the great beast? Were they protecting themselves by recreating its image?

"I hammered three times on the door with my fist. After about two minutes a voice came from within, 'State your business!' I called out and explained that I was a lone traveller, that I was on my way north to Albion and I wanted to work for food and water. There was silence and then suddenly the door began to open. Standing there was a boy with a strange headdress. It was made of twigs and grass and just like the carvings on the gate, it was very crude but it did have a passing resemblance to the head and neck of a dragon!

His face was muddy and he looked afraid. He was around 20 years old but the lines on his face made him look older. Aside from his headdress he was dressed in sackcloth, and was barefoot. He looked half-starved but somehow pleased to see me. He did not say anything but just stood there looking me up and down until his eyes met mine. His mouth fell open and he seemed to be in a state of shock and I did not know what to say or do. Then from behind him I heard a voice saying, 'Who is this woman?' in an accent that I recognised from a long time ago. Looking to the boy's left, I saw him. He too was wearing a strange head dress and a basic sack cloth tunic. He was looking at me with blue eyes just like mine. He was tall and did not look as thin and unwell as the boy who had opened the gate, who by now had pulled himself together and was looking from me to the other man with a look of confusion and excitement on his face and said 'Master Ddraig, her eyes are the same as yours! Is this woman your true kin?'

"Ignoring the boy the man looked right at me and said 'What is your name lady?' I looked at him and he did not look as if he was in anyway angry and I did not feel as if I was in any kind of danger. However I did feel as if this man knew me and I could not think of any reason not to tell him my name and so looking him in the eye, I simply said my name was Morgana.

"The man did not move. It was as if time had stood still. Looking at me he asked me again 'What is your name lady?' and again I told him. Then something happened that I did not expect. He took my two hands in his and fell to his knees and then looking up at me he said the words that I would never forget: 'I am just like you, I am one of your people and I too survived the day the great beast came to kills us all, I, like you, have lived for a very long time, I have travelled all over this world trying to find the origins of the creature that destroyed everything we loved!'

"I could not speak or move and his words for a moment did not register in my mind and I could not bring myself to believe what this man was saying to me.

"Standing up and letting go of my hands he looked over to the boy who had opened the gate to me and told him to go and collect firewood and he would speak to him later and he did so without hesitation.

"As you can imagine I had so many questions for this strange man. Who was he? Why was he living like this?

"He said he was one of my people but to my eyes he was a stranger and I had never seen him before that day but, apart from the fact that his eyes were as blue as mine, I somehow knew that he and I were the same and came from the same place and indeed the same time.

"He seemed to know what I was thinking and asked me to follow him to a small run down little hut near the gate and I did so without fear for I trusted him but I did not know why.

"He invited me to sit down and he told me a tale that was both informative and exciting. I did not make any attempt to interrupt him as he spoke.

"He told me that on the day our home was destroyed he had been little more than a child and was left for dead but somehow and in some way he survived. He could not tell me how but he knew that our people lived for a very long time and as far as he knew we could not die by any means other than by the fire from a dragon. He told me that over the years he had heard rumours of a woman travelling alone on this continent with eyes as blue as his own but made no move to find out more because he wanted to find the true origins of the dragon in the hope of stopping it from killing anyone else.

"Looking at me as we sat in the shabby hut he said 'I first travelled to the east of this continent after being told by some slave traders that a great beast had been seen near the town of Moskva that stands on a frozen river and when I got there the people told me that indeed they had seen a winged monster that came from the far east. I knew what I had to do next and as much as it took me three years I made it to what the people of that land called the Middle Kingdom a very long way from here and it was here that I found what I was looking for. I knew that there must be a way of stopping all the killing and destruction and there must be someone out there who knew how this could be done.

"The land of the middle kingdom was vast and its people looked somewhat different to the people of this land but never the less they were happy to talk with me. I learnt their language and their ways and soon they come to trust me. News of me even reached the Emperor of this land. His name was Qin Shi Huang and he sent word that he wished to meet with me; so came the day that I was presented to the Emperor. We talked for a long time and he wanted to know who I was and why I had come so far to visit his land.

I told him that I wanted to find out where the dragon came from. I told him that I had been told that it came from this part of the world. He told me that when he was a child he had seen a dragon fly across the sky but that was long ago and it was the only time, but he knew of them and told me that the king of Bhutan once told him that the only way to keep a dragon away was to make it forever sleep and the only way to do that was to display its image far and wide for a dragon cannot be killed by anything at all. He went on to tell me that each year the people of his country would hold festivals on both land and water and the people would make great models and lanterns in the shape of dragons and parade with them across the land in the hope that no dragons would be seen in the skies.

"The Emperor went on to tell me that his people did the same and that each year the same kind of parade was held in the hope of keeping the dragon asleep. Where the dragon slept, how many there were or why its image kept it asleep he could not say but he also saw to it that its image was seen throughout his kingdom.

Great statues were built and its image could be seen everywhere and its image could be found in artwork and painted upon pottery, although it's image differed somewhat from the images I have seen on this continent in essence they were the same.

"I thanked the Emperor and made up my mind to travel to the kingdom of Bhutan - a country to the north that the people called the Land of the Thunder Dragon. I wanted to understand why the image of the dragon would keep the real thing at bay.

"My journey north was not an easy one, the people I met in the remote areas were suspicious of me and they did not welcome strangers but I did not give up and at last after many weeks I made it to The Land of the Thunder Dragon.

"The land was mountainous and the architecture was very different to anything I had ever seen. Its people were for the most part friendly, and I spoke with many of them. They all knew of the dragon and I saw its imagery everywhere from statues to jewellery. It seemed to me that the dragon was a major part of their culture. Songs were sang about dragons and poems were written in the form of warnings to anyone who did not display its image. I remember one specifically and although it doesn't really rhyme very well I will also remember it.......

"In the land of the Thunder Dragon and within the greatest peak sleeps the nemesis to our peace, its potent hatred and arrogance must forever slumber, for our land would perish in destruction and flame. Its image and symbol must be forever seen to keep the creature within its dreams."

"The poem although short told me a great deal and one thing that was for sure to see that the dragon forever slept was to make and display its form but I still did not understand why this was so until one day I was sitting alone high on a cliff top looking out at a Great mountain in the distance, and from behind me I heard footsteps. Turning and standing up I saw a young woman. She approached gently and to my astonishment she introduced herself as the Princess of Bhutan. I then told her that my name was Ddraig and it was indeed an honour to meet her.

"She told me that she had come on the orders of her father the king to give me the answers that I was seeking. I knew that before the day was over I would know everything about dragons and hopefully how to stop them killing and destroying. We talked for a very long time and she told me that dragons were not always monstrous but it was loneliness that made them turn to violence.

"They were lonely because there were so few of them left in the world. She also told me that they were once proud and noble creatures but the pride had turned to arrogance and spite.

I asked her how she knew all of this and she told me that in the past her people had been living with the threat for many years and so many of her people dedicated themselves to the study of these creatures, in fact her home land was called The Land of the Thunder Dragon because the roar of the dragon sounded like thunder.

"She told me that an ancient King decided that his people had lived in the shadow of fear for long enough and realising that the dragon was prideful and arrogant he ordered that a great cave in the side of a mountain be used to capture the dragon and so all the people worked together and inside the cave carved images everywhere for the king knew in his wisdom that the dragon would, in its pride, come to see what had been done, and years later it did so. The story goes that it flew into the mountain and saw what it considered to be a tribute to its greatness and so feeling contented it fell asleep, and over time there were earthquakes and landslides that resulted in the entrance to the cave being sealed forever with the dragon asleep inside. I then asked her where this mountain could be found, and smiling she pointed into the distance to the very mountain I was looking at just before she approached.

"I thanked her and she told me to go back to my own land and people and make preparations so should a dragon ever be seen in my part of the world I would know what to do.

"I left the next day for I now had the answers I wanted and I longed for home!"

"The years passed and I finally made it back to this continent and I found that it had changed very little. I lived in the Black Forest to the east. I saw no one for a very long time until one day I ran into a group of nomads.

They were gathering supplies in the forest and they were happy for me to talk with them and stay with them for a time and as much as they were simple people I enjoyed their company but then one day as we were sitting around a fire there came a great gust of wind that scattered and put out the fire. I looked up and there in the sky above the trees was a great red dragon! It was a colossal size! Where it came from I could not say and to this very day I still do not know! I knew at once what had to be done but I knew of no great cave into which I could tempt the creature and so I told the group of terrified nomads the story that the Princess in Bhutan had told me years before and as much as there was no cave there were trees in to which its image could be carved and so we travelled many miles to find the right place to do our work. After much searching we found a large clearing surrounded by trees and we went to work on them. Into hundreds of trees we carved an image of a dragon. We worked for many weeks and when it was done I sent the nomadic people away. I told them to make for the coast and that in time I would find them.

"The months went by and I stayed at the clearing until one evening as the sun was setting it returned as I knew it would. I saw it land in the clearing and it's eyes were studying the carvings in the trees and then quite suddenly it laid down and to my astonishment and great relief it went to sleep. I felt a great feeling of optimism that this dragon would stay here and just like the Thunder Dragon in the kingdom of Bhutan it would forever sleep and as far as I know it is still there.
   It has been 20 years and I can only hope that the great beast has been covered in falling leaves and hidden from view.'

It was also evident that Ddraig had spent many years living in this rundown fortress with people who had for a very long time wandered the land in search for food, but had suddenly become static and that may well explain why they were living in what really amounted to squalor.

Morgana however knew exactly what she was going to do. Surrounding the settlement there were hundreds and hundreds of wooden stakes that made up the tall fence and they could be put to much better use in the building of a boat that, if made properly, could carry all of them across the sea to the mysterious land of Albion.

Morgana knew it would be a difficult task, persuading Ddraig to dismantle the settlement and leave it altogether to travel north across the sea. Persuading the nomadic tribe who lived inside this fortress, however, was not very difficult at all for it was in their nature to not stay in one place for very long.

When she informed them of her idea and intention, each and every one of them seemed enthusiastic at the thought of moving on again, even if it was across the sea to an unknown land.

After much persuasion, Ddraig finally agreed and so the work began in dismantling the great fence that surrounded the shabby hamlet and through there was a great deal of trial and error Morgana, Ddraig and the nomads finally built a boat that was seaworthy.

The crossing took two days but the sea was calm and everybody on board worked hard with his or her oar until finally in the distance, across the sea, great white cliffs began to grow bigger and bigger.

In her heart Morgana knew that this was the land of Albion and that a new chapter in her life was about to begin. This was the land that she had longed for. This was the land that she knew she belonged to. This was to be her home for evermore. She did not know where or how she was going to live or what perils lay in wait for her. What were the people that lived on this island like?

Did they welcome strangers?

Were there ferocious wild animals?

All of these things did not at that moment matter at all, for at that moment as the great white cliffs of this mysterious land loomed over the small boat, Morgana knew that after thousands of years she was again home.

After some searching they found an inlet and pulled the boat up a sandy beach where they camped for the night and in the morning it was time to make plans and decide what to do next. The nomadic people numbered around 60 men, women and children and they more than Ddraig were excited at the prospect of exploring a new land and so they decided, somewhat reluctantly, to set off that very morning in search of new and exciting territory to explore. They no longer had their dragon-like headdresses, but each and every one of them had tied around their necks a clay model of a dragon that Ddraig had given to them before the voyage, in the hope that it may protect them should the dragon ever come to these shores. They all said goodbye to both Morgana and Ddraig, and left to begin a new life in a land that they and their descendants would call home.

Both Morgana and Ddraig were left standing quite alone on a sandy beach as it started to rain. Looking at each other they both knew that it was time for them to also part ways. They were both so used to their independence that it would not do to travel together and explore this new land. They both knew that they would see each other again in the future but for now it was time to separate.

The years passed by, and Morgana by now was living alone some miles from where the boat had landed. She was living a happy but simple life. She had built herself a comfortable home and set up a small farm and traded nuts, fruits and vegetables with the native peoples of the island in return for the things she needed.

The native people of Albion were, for the most part peaceful and did not interfere with Morgana and she in turn did not do anything to disturb their natural progression or beliefs.

Although she spent a great deal of time trying to discover if a dragon or anything like it had ever been seen on this island, she didn't discover any evidence that the people of this land had ever seen or indeed heard of such a thing.

But over the years as the world matured, trickles of stories reached the island from the lands across the sea and in time the dragon, although seen mostly as a mythical creature, became part of stories and folklore in Albion.

Chapter 12
The Dig

It was late at night and Morgana was asleep in her small dwelling when a rustling sound outside made her wake up. It was very dark and through that darkness there came the words "Morgana are you in there?" This was a voice she hadn't heard in over 150 years. It was the voice of her old friend Ddraig.

Getting out of bed and opening the door Morgana was surprised to see Ddraig and invited him in. They talked for hours, and by the time they had finished the sun had risen. He told her that after they parted he travelled right across the island, met many different people and then finally settled in the far north in the land of the Pics and devoted the next 30 years or so to writing a book. Handing it to her he said "I have written down in this book all my knowledge regarding dragons and I want you to have it. It has taken me many years to find you and now that I have I must again say goodbye to you, for I now intend to leave this island and travel the world again. If we do meet again it will not be for a very, very long time."

And without saying anything else he simply kissed Morgana on both cheeks and left. Morgana for her part was not surprised at this behaviour and did not question it.

Ddraig and Morgana never met again, although Morgana did from time to time think about him, she knew that wherever he was and whatever he was doing it was for the greater good of all people for he was a good and honest man. In the days to come she read the book that Ddraig had given to her; it, of course, was the same book that the Prince had found in his library just days before.

Morgana explained to the Royal Family that she had kept the book safe for over a thousand years. She told them of how she had seen the Roman Empire rise and fall on this island, and how during its height she had met one of the Roman imperial governors and he gave her the rights and ownership of the mountain she now lived in the shadow of. As for the book, the day came when Aled (the first warrior prince of South Wales) was proclaimed ruler of that land and it was to him Morgana gave the book and in doing so started the tradition of presenting gifts to the new ruler of south Wales on his or her coronation day, a tradition that has lasted for the last 250 years. Eventually a great library was built as part of his castle and there, on one of its dusty shelves, the book was placed, ignored and forgotten until just days ago when the descendent of the first warrior Prince Aled of South Wales took it down and read it from cover to cover.

From that day Morgana got to know each ruler of South Wales and without exception she was proud of all of them. She of course out lived each of them and was deeply saddened when each of them died, however the kingdom they left was indeed a fine and prosperous land and its people were happy and prosperous because of it.

Morgana lived happily and peacefully at the mountain for a very long time. She did not mingle or interact with the people very much and preferred instead to live mostly in solitude. Occasionally however, she liked to visit the town and she would walk there on a sunny day. During these outings she enjoyed seeing the men working in the fields and the children playing in the streams. Inside the walled town she would make conversation with the local people and buy the things she needed from the market. It was during one of these visits she was passing the work shop of the stonemason and sculptor. This man was a true artist and he was busy chipping away at a great piece of stone with a hammer and chisel. The great stone was white in colour. The stonemason was chiselling at what looked to be the face and neck of a dragon. Its mouth was open and a great tongue was protruding.

Morgana stopped and stared at this creature with wonder. It had been a very long time since she had seen the image of a dragon. Her curiosity got the better of her and she politely started a conversation with the stonemason. He was a kind and cheerful man and welcomed a short break from his work and invited Morgana to sit down.

They both chatted for some time until Morgana asked him about his fine creation and he told her that he was carving this mythological creature at the request of Princess Angharad, who at that time was the ruler of South Wales. She was the great-great-great grandmother of the current Prince. She was a strong and just ruler; she made good laws and encouraged the people of South Wales to educate themselves through reading and writing. She opened schools and made the education of children compulsory.

She had one young son and he, like all the children in the kingdom, spent five days a week being educated but this boy did not go to school, the school came to him.

Each day a teacher was called to the palace and educated the young prince in reading and writing, Mathematics and Science but above all things his favourite subject to study was by far History, and not just the history of South Wales but the entire island and the rest of the known world.

The boy's teacher was a very kind man, if not a little unusual. Around his neck on a gold chain was an ancient small clay model of a dragon. He would tell the young prince all kinds of stories and legends about great beasts called dragons that could breathe fire, and the little boy thoroughly enjoyed them and so for his 13th birthday he asked his mother for a statue of a dragon to be placed in the courtyard of the Castle. The statue would be modelled on the small clay version that belonged to the Prince's teacher.

It was a safe bet to assume that the schoolteacher was in fact a descendent of the nomadic people who came to what was then called Albion many hundreds of years before with Morgana and Ddraig

The young prince loved the stories so much that his mother ordered that the myths and legends concerning dragons be taught in every school throughout the kingdom. She felt quite rightly that it was important for young people to enjoy fantastical stories and that is why the people of the kingdom knew all about dragons but up until that week most did not think they were real things that could kill you!

Morgana and the Royal Family eventually went to bed and in the morning the Prince asked that Morgana meet with him again, for he still had many questions. The both of them were sitting in the Great Hall of the castle and the Prince was the first to raise the question regarding making an alliance with the kingdoms to the west and to the north. He voiced his concerns and told Morgana that making an alliance with Uther Pendragon would be dangerous and no doubt almost impossible. He told her that the Northern Queen believed Uther was to blame for the dragon awakening. He also raised concerns around the fact that he did not trust or ever like Uther or the Northern Queen.

Morgana up until now did not speak. She was looking at the Prince with pride and compassion for she knew he was a good and brave man who would gladly lay down his life for his people.

She then smiled and said, "My Prince, today you must send messages to The Queen of the North and to Uther Pendragon and ask for soldiers and as many man each kingdom can provide, but you do not need their swords or spears. You do not need their bows and arrows. No, you do not need their weapons. You must inform the rulers of both these lands that the men they send must bring with them pickaxes and shovels and anything else they may have to dig with.

As I told you before, there is no weapon on earth that can kill a dragon and the only way to be free of it is to make it sleep forever." The Prince opened his mouth to speak but Morgana put up her hand and continued, "Also, this day you must send out messengers to every corner of your kingdom to inform all the people that each and every one who is able must make a model of the dragon and bring it here to the castle at once.

It doesn't matter how detailed it is or even its size, but each person must make some kind of model or likeness of the dragon. You must also tell the blacksmiths not to bother about making extra weapons, but to put all their effort into making digging equipment such as shovels and pickaxes. The only way we are going to defeat this dragon is to dig a great hole in my mountain and fill it with all manner of images and models that resembles the dragon!

"As I told you last night, long ago a king in the Kingdom of Bhutan ordered something similar to be done and it seemed to have worked and we must try and do that here very soon.

Again as I told you last night, a long time ago I came into possession of that mountain and I did so because I knew that the day would come that the very same dragon that destroyed my people would rise again and destroy everything it saw! It is now completely irrelevant who is responsible for waking the dragon from its sleep. What matters now is that we act quickly. It is my understanding that you have called all able-bodied men to the castle and that all the kingdoms officials are present?" To this the Prince did not comment and simply nodded and Morgana went on and said, "My advice to you now my Prince is that you call a council of your officials and tell them what needs to be done. A great hole must be dug into my mountain to trap the dragon and make it forever sleep and so I suggest you put all those strong able-bodied men to work at once and as many men from the army as possible must do the same."

The rest of the day was truly incredible. Each of the kingdoms officials worked incredibly hard organising what were not preparations for battle but a massive undertaking to dig a great pit at the top of a Mountain!

There was a great deal of commotion across the land. The men that came in to the town to fight were now making their way to the mountain, each of them carrying a spade or a pickaxe and each one determined to do all they could to complete what seemed to be an almost impossible task.

The prince also sent ambassadors to the courts of the Northern Queen and of Uther Pendragon. He gave them orders to tell both rulers exactly what was going on and exactly what was at stake and it was imperative that each ruler send men and digging equipment as soon as possible! If indeed it was down to Uther Pendragon that the dragon was now free it didn't really matter at the moment. What mattered now was dealing with it.

The prince also did what Morgana suggested and sent messengers to every corner of the kingdom giving orders that each citizen make some kind of model of the dragon and bring them to the castle as soon as possible.

The Prince and his family were working very hard. The four young Princesses were organising food for the men who were digging. The Prince and his wife spent every day at the mountain doing all they could do to encourage the men with their very difficult task.

The Prince himself too spent hours at a time digging alongside his men.

The hole had to be bigger than the dragon itself for a great many models of it were to be put inside in the hope that the beast would simply fly inside.

Over the coming days a great many models of the dragon arrived in the town. They were of all shapes and sizes. They were made of clay and wood. Some too were made of twigs and grass, others carved from stone.

The Prince ordered that the great stone statue of the dragon that was in the courtyard of the castle be brought to the mountain in readiness to be placed in the great hole next to all the others.

The weather was getting colder but this did not do anything to discourage anyone and after around six days the great hole was half done, but the men of the kingdom were becoming exhausted and more help was needed and quickly.

The Prince was sitting on the grass resting with some of his men. He had just spent the last four hours digging when a messenger approached and handed him a piece of paper. It was from the captain of the second regiment who was in charge of guarding the western border of South Wales and on it were written the words, *"My Prince, there are around 4000 men at the border. They tell me they are here at your request and on the orders of their king Uther Pendragon. They wish to join in the work at the mountain."*

The Prince was astonished at the words he was reading and knowing that 4000 extra men would indeed be a great help he ordered the messenger to return at once to the western border and informed the good captain there to not only thank the men for coming but to escort them to the mountain as soon as possible.

It was evident that the ambassador that was sent to the court of Uther Pendragon was successful, this news was met with enthusiasm, relief and some suspicion by the Prince. On the one hand 4000 extra pairs of hands would be welcomed by all the kingdom, but on the other hand 4000 men was an army and as much as the army of South Wales were far greater in number, this amount of men from West Wales was a potential threat to the kingdom. However, the Prince was a trusting man and as long as they remained peaceful and did what was asked of them there would not be any problems.

It would take a day or two for the 4000 men to reach the mountain. And so it gave the Prince the time and the opportunity to put certain security measures in place.

He spoke in length with the General, explaining the need for tight security but from a strict distance. He wanted the men from West Wales to feel welcome.

The following day was much the same. More and more models of the dragon floated into the town and to everybody's surprise, around 200 rather tired and scruffy men from the Northern Kingdom turned up with shovels, on the orders of their Queen. They were very shy and didn't really speak to anyone at all. The eldest of the Princesses made it her mission to see that they were fed and looked after during their work on the mountain.

Each man worked hard all day and by now great mounds of earth were appearing around the mouth to the great hole, and long ladders were being used to get in and out.

Each man would fill a large bucket and physically carry it out of the hole. Morgana asked the Prince to leave the earth where it was for she hoped that the time would come when the dragon was safely sleeping inside the hole, all the earth could be placed back on top of the dragon. Although it would not suffocate it, for nothing on this earth can kill a dragon, it would at least hide it away and in doing so prevent anyone from disturbing it forever more.

There was a great feeling of optimism at the dig site. Thousands of people gathered at the top of the mountain. The men were digging the hole and the women were taking the buckets and emptying the earth safely around the edge.

The youngest of the Prince's daughters began to make preparations and organising all the models and images of the dragon to be brought to the mountain and for this she asked the children and young people of the Kingdom to help when the time was right and the digging was completed.

Everything was going to plan, and with the arrival of another 4000 men from the western kingdom the following day, the completion of the task seemed assured and if every man, woman and child did their best the task would be completed in around seven days.

When the dragon would appear was of course not known but Morgana was confident that it would not be long, and she was confident that the plan would work. She knew how deadly and dangerous the dragon was and the absolute importance of the work they were doing.

Chapter 13
The Fall of a Kingdom

As the days went by the 4000 men from the western kingdom worked hard alongside everyone else. They were strong, and only stopped work to eat and sleep. They did not mix with anyone but just got on with the digging.

The work on the great pit was finished within six days and then the countless models of all shapes and sizes of the dragon were brought to the mountain by the young people of the kingdom and one by one placed in the pit along with the great dragon statue that had stood in the castle courtyard.

That night there was a great celebration on the side of the mountain. Bonfires were lit and there was singing, dancing and feasting and the people of South Wales rejoiced at what they had achieved, not only for themselves but for all the peoples of Wales and beyond. The men from the Northern realm joined in with the celebrations but the 4000 men from West Wales simply gathered together and prepared to sleep. The Prince was disappointed by this and requested to speak to their leader and representative. He was a man that worked just as hard and anyone else. He was tall and thick set. His eyes were brown and his face did not seem to show any emotion of any kind. When he was presented to the Prince they talked for some time. The Prince again thanked him and his men on behalf of the entire kingdom.

The man simply said he was doing his duty on the orders of his king and that when the dragon was finally in the pit he and his men would leave for West Wales. He politely told the Prince that his men would not be joining the celebrations and what they needed now was rest. The Prince reluctantly accepted this and told the man to re-join his men and have a good night's sleep.

The celebrations continued until dawn. As the sun began to rise and the great bonfires began to fizzle out, Morgana was walking towards the edge of the great pit. She too had been celebrating with the people. She above everyone else knew how important this great work had been and she knew that it was the only way to keep the entire island safe.

It was a very cold morning and the people began packing away their belongings to leave the mountain. It was now a waiting game. Nobody could say for sure when the dragon would arrive but suddenly there was a great guest of wind. Morgana and everyone else who was on the mountain saw it. It was a colossal size. Its wings were huge and its eyes were as black as coal!

The Dragon had arrived! The people began to panic and run in every direction. They began to fall over each other as they ran down the mountain. Only the Prince, the Princess, their four daughters and a handful of brave soldiers along with Morgana stood their ground.

The 4000 men from the western kingdom did not seem to react in the same way as everybody else and they simply picked up their tools and quietly walked down the mountainside.

The dragon by now was circling around the mountain. It was watching everything that was going on. It made no move to harm anyone and then suddenly it began to dive towards the mountain. The Prince and the others flung themselves upon the ground but the dragon took no notice of them and what followed was totally remarkable. The great beast simply flew into the pit. It stood for a moment at the bottom and looked around at its surroundings and at all the carvings and sculptures and then simply laid down and quite peacefully went to sleep.

Morgana was the first to get to her feet and eventually getting to the edge of the pit. She looked inside and there she saw the great dragon that was responsible for destroying everything she knew and loved so long ago asleep in the bottom of a massive hole. The Prince was next to arrive, and then his family and a hand full of soldiers.

Each of them looked with astonishment into the great pit. The dragon seemed sound asleep. It was truly enormous and each of them could not seem to take their eyes off it until suddenly Morgana stepped forward picked up a muddy rock that was lying on the ground and threw it at the slumbering beast. It did not move a muscle. She then turned to the Prince and said, "Now is the time to fill in the pit. Now, my Prince is the time to cover the dragon in earth, although it will not suffocate or die. It will sleep and the people of this land will be safe!" The Prince quickly turned to the soldiers and told them to call the people back to the top of the mountain for there was more work to be done!

So again the work began. Thousands and thousands of the people who had spent a great deal of time digging a great hole now began to fill it again. Huge amounts of earth were placed on top of the sleeping dragon and by night fall the task was complete.

The Prince called the people together on top of what was now a great mound of earth and by flaming torch light he gave a speech and told the people that they should be incredibly proud of themselves and to never forget what could be achieved by working together. He told them that no Prince anywhere in the world could be more proud than he was that night.

As the people again began to celebrate by singing and dancing something quite different was happening many miles away at the borders of the kingdom.

The Prince did not at any time neglect the boundaries of his land and saw to it that they were guarded in the same way as they had always been but the soldiers there were in for a terrible shock. For at precisely 7 o'clock all three borders of the kingdom, that is to say the border with the kingdom of West Wales, the border with North Wales and the borders with the Anglo-Saxon kingdom, were suddenly and simultaneously attacked by tens of thousands of soldiers.

Legions of soldiers overwhelmed the western defences. Three regiments of Anglo-Saxon warriors completely destroyed the fortifications at the eastern border and countless soldiers from North Wales overwhelmed the northern defences and poured into South Wales.

The soldiers protecting the borders were completely taken by surprise and stood little chance in the face of such numbers!

The outlying villages were the first to fall and all the people could do was run! Just an hour later three larger towns were attacked and as much as the townspeople put up a courageous fight they too were overwhelmed!

Meanwhile at Caerphilly mountain the Prince and his family were preparing to leave and return to the castle, for no one there knew of what was happening elsewhere in the kingdom, when suddenly out of nowhere came the voice of the man everyone had thought to be the leader of the men who were sent by North Wales to help with the digging. He was shouting the words "Obey your king! Attack! Attack!" This was no ordinary man! He wasn't just one of the workers; he was in fact Uther Pendragon, King and ruler of West Wales!

Suddenly the 4000 of his men as well as those from north Wales who were still at the mountain with everybody else pulled out swords that they had kept secretly concealed under their clothes and began to attack anyone who happened to be close by!

There was a great deal of confusion and commotion. There were people screaming and running in every direction! Within minutes the soldiers of South Wales that were present surrounded the Prince and his family but it was no good!

There were still too many of them! The Prince and his family were unarmed for they never felt the need to carry weapons inside the kingdom. Morgana, who saw what was going on, quickly stepped forward and took hold of the youngest of the Prince's daughters by the arm and told her to quickly gather her sisters and follow her! The girl at once did what she was told and within minutes all five of them were running down the mountain and out of sight. Fierce fighting broke out and the Prince battled courageously even though he had no sword of his own!

His eldest daughter, who was running away, stopped for a moment and looked back and she saw something that filled her with absolute terror. Her father was lying on the ground. He was dead!

He had been killed fighting to protect his wife! She began to scream but Morgana running back towards her took her by the arm and pulled her away, telling her that she must join her sisters for she too could be killed!! Reluctantly she did what she was told and all five of them ran and ran until they reached Morgana's house at the foot of the mountain. Morgana pushed all four Princesses in through the door and told them to stay inside and not to move until her return. All four of them were in great distress but did as they were told.

The fighting had become fierce and fearing for the Prince's wife four of the Princes soldiers took hold of her and more or less dragged her away she protested and ordered the men to let her go. She was a brave woman and she wanted to fight for her country and her people. She knew that her husband was dead and that her four daughters were safe for the moment with Morgana, but it was no good, the kingdom was about to fall!

The loyal soldiers persuaded the Princess to get on a horse and ride to the coast. She knew that there was no alternative and so with three soldiers and no belongings she did what they suggested. Within an hour she was standing on the deck of a sailboat and was about to sail away from the land she loved. Her husband was dead, her home was in chaos and her four daughters would now have to grow up without a mother and father.

Her story, although very sad, did not end here and the time would come when she would find happiness again but that is another story.

Morgana did not return to her house that night, and the four Princesses did not see anyone. They knew that their father was dead but they had no idea what had become of their mother and the rest of the kingdom.

The following day there was still no news and they started to worry about Morgana but she had been very busy indeed. She had put on the disguise of a milkmaid and went on a fact finding mission.

The entire kingdom was completely over run and she learnt from two men who had been hiding in a barn that Uther Pendragon had declared himself king of South Wales. They told her that they had heard from others that the now king had entered secretly into an alliance with the Northern Queen and the Anglo-Saxons to take South Wales by force after the great dragon had been subdued.

It was their belief that he had purposely sent agents to awaken the dragon from across the sea so that the Prince would put all his efforts in to dealing with it and most likely ask him for help and in doing so he had the perfect opportunity to send 4000 men deep into South Wales and in doing so not only speeded up the digging of the great pit but also had the devastating effect of having soldiers both inside and outside of the South Wales.

Morgana completely agreed that this was the most likely scenario.

She also found out what happened to the Princes' wife. A soldier she knew who was also in disguise told her that she had been put on a sailboat and safely taken away across the sea.

There was one last thing that she wanted to do before she returned to the four young Princesses and that was to see the Royal Castle for the last time, for she knew that it would be completely destroyed because it symbolised the authority of its dead ruler.

However by the time she had got there it was already being demolished. The new king had given orders that it be completely destroyed. What's more, he wanted any and all symbols that represented the conquered Royal house to be thrown into the river Taff at various points along its path!

Morgana knew that all was now lost and the Kingdom as she knew it was gone.

On her journey home back to her small house at the foot of the mountain she was told by some arrogant soldiers from West Wales that a great deal of land to the North of the now conquered kingdom had been given to the Queen of North Wales and the same to the Anglo-Saxons to the east.

The four Princesses were sitting at the table. They were grief stricken, confused and terrified. Everything and everyone they knew and loved was either gone or destroyed - what would become of them? Their father was betrayed and dead, their mother gone across the sea, forced into a boat by some well meaning loyal soldiers. The entire kingdom was overrun by Anglo-

Saxons and the army had been defeated. The people faced a cruel future of oppression.

Their future looked bleak indeed and all four of them sat in the little house next to the mountain and remained silent for what seemed like hours.

The sun had set and the only light in the kitchen came from the one candle that the youngest daughter lit and placed in the middle of the table.

Suddenly in the silence the sound of footsteps could be heard outside the door. All four daughters looked at each other. The youngest silently got to her feet blew out the candle and picked up her chair above her head and walked silently to the door. She was ready to bring the heavy chair down on the head of any Anglo-Saxon who dared to open the door!

The other three backed into a corner and held their breath. The door slowly opened and the youngest daughter was ready to defend her three sisters! As the door opened a hand came around it and on the second finger was a silver ring with a white stone that luckily the youngest daughter recognised and so put down the chair. Morgana came in to the room. She was carrying a lantern. Although she was smiling her eyes were wide and bright, her hair was windswept and the bottom of her cloak was wet and muddy and after she put her staff against the wall she turned and locked the door, closed the shutters on the kitchen window and then turned to the four Princesses and said "Please sit, for we have a great deal to discuss. I know your hearts are heavy with grief and I know you are frightened and confused but we have very little time. I promise no one will come here tonight but by morning we must leave this house and get away from here." All four of them looked at her in astonishment- where were they going?

The kingdom had fallen and Uther Pendragon was now king of most of South Wales. Great swathes of land to the north of the kingdom had been given to the decadent selfish Queen who had allied herself with Uther and the rest of Britain was overrun with Anglo-Saxons.

The second daughter asked the question that they were all thinking: "Where can we go lady? Where is safe for us?" All four of them were looking at Morgana for reassurance and help.

The answer she gave was to them totally unacceptable. She told them that the only way the four of them could survive was to separate. She explained that it wasn't safe for all four of them to stay together in South Wales. As she spoke each daughter protested. They had lost their parents, the kingdom they loved so much had been conquered, but to be separated from each other too was simply out of the question! But the more Morgana spoke, the more she impressed on them that the new King would not rest until they were found and imprisoned or worse, and so they began to realise that what she was saying was for the best and for now at least it would be better and indeed safer if they were all to separate.

The hours passed and Morgana prepared a small meal. Slowly their plan of escape came together. It was important that everything was planned meticulously for nothing could be left to chance.

As they talked Morgana told them that it was essential that in the years to come the image of the dragon should be seen right across all Wales and it was up to them to pass this important fact on to their children and see that they did the same. "Can you promise me that you can do this? She ask the four girls for The Dragon will only sleep if it thinks that all know of its existence!"

After more discussion and planning it was decided by all concerned that the eldest Princess was to stay in South Wales. She would make a home away from the castle. She knew of a place some 25 miles away by the sea. There was a small village and she knew she would be safe there. The people would protect her and keep her secret. She couldn't bring herself to leave her beloved South Wales. It was indeed part of her and leaving it would truly break her heart.

The second daughter would travel to the Anglo-Saxon stronghold of London. She quite rightly assumed that London was the last place anyone would think to look for her. She would take a job as a maid-servant or the like. It would be nothing like the life she was used to but it would be a safe and peaceful one.

The third daughter decided to go to Portsmouth.

It was a busy port and she would find work there without too much difficulty. There she could live out her days and maybe even with a little contentment.

The fourth daughter it was decided would travel to the West Midlands and become a farmer. She was indeed a fearless girl. She could wield a sword as good as any man but for now it was best to live a quiet peaceful life in obscurity.

Three out of the four Princes' daughters would leave Wales all with a burning determination to one day return. The feeling of loss and sadness was suffocating but suddenly the talking stopped and the four of them suddenly came to the realisation that their elder sister was indeed the true and rightful ruler of all South Wales. Their father was dead and now their sister was the true Princess Regent of the Kingdom! Morgana, realising what they were thinking, said "My dear friends, from this night on you must put your old lives behind you. Your royal titles are now dangerous. You must never reveal your true identity to anyone you do not trust absolutely, but never forget who you are." Looking at the eldest daughter she said "You my dear are the true and rightful ruler of this land and you must never forget that or what I told you all." Smiling she got up from the table. It was the early hours of the morning. Morgana gave her bed to the two youngest daughters. The other two made themselves comfortable on two armchairs in the other room and soon all four were asleep.

Morgana spent the next few hours packing up provisions for the four Princesses.

When the morning came and the sun had risen, Morgana gently woke them up and after a large breakfast it was time to go. In a small field behind the house there were five horses that belonged to Morgana. Each Princess chose a horse and mounted. They gathered on horseback in front of the house where Morgana was standing.

She was looking up to them and said "My dear brave Princesses, you have shown that you are indeed your father's daughters. Like him you are kind, brave and just. You have shown considerable resilience against all you have suffered. Both your father and mother would be incredibly proud of you."

The four Princesses looked at her and each other with mixed feelings of pride and sadness. They knew that their old lives had ended and on that chilly morning in South Wales they were about to start anew but only this time they would be separated from each other and they didn't know when or indeed if they would meet again.

"I have one last thing to tell you before you must leave." Morgana came closer to them and said "Your father's ancestors denied themselves the title of King or Queen because they did not want to hold such a lofty and ostentatious title. They, like your good father, showed great humility and love for the people of South Wales."

She smiled and looked down at the silver ring on her finger. The unusual stone seemed to shine in the morning sun and looking up in the faces of the four Princesses. She said, "You know that I am of a great age and I have lived here for a very long time and I know your father was the direct descendent of a man that long ago ruled this land on behalf of a great Emperor from across the sea and he like your father was a man of peace and indeed a man of and for the people and his blood now flows in your veins." The youngest Princess was about to ask a question but Morgana raised her hand and said gently; "My dear Princess there is no time for questions. I know that things seem bleak now but I know in my heart that you will be prosperous in the years to come. You all, I am sure, will fall in love and marry. Should you be blessed with children they too will have your father's blood running in their veins and to them you can tell your stories." The Princesses looked at each other in confusion but did not ask any more questions. "It is now time to go. I will stay here for the rest of the morning and then I will leave for the hills."

As she said this she pointed in what seemed to be a random direction but the Princesses did not comment.

Looking up at the four of them Morgana said, "Nothing is ever as bad as you think it's going to be, not when it comes to it, you remember that." She smiled and then turned without saying goodbye, walked into the house and closed the door behind her.

The four Princesses were astonished at this abrupt exit but knew it was time to depart. All four of them made a solemn promise that one day and in better times they would meet again, and just as it began to rain they departed and separated for their own destinations across Britain. They did not know it but that was the very last time they would ever see each other, but they did not forget each other or who they were.

The years passed by and South Wales became a black shadow of what it used to be. Uther Pendragon was a tyrannical king. He taxed the people heavily and with his Anglo-Saxon army he ruled with an iron fist. The people who were once prosperous now eked out a living on small farms and smallholdings.

The four Princesses did however prosper. The first as we know stayed in South Wales, and she married and had twin sons.

The second travelled to London and set up home and worked as a servant. She married a man who came each week to her master's house to collect the rubbish.

He was a good man and together they had two daughters and just like her three sisters she kept her promise to pass the story of her previous life down to her children.

The third daughter travelled to Portsmouth. She too married. Her husband was a blacksmith, and she had six children.

The fourth daughter also left Wales altogether and travelled to the West Midlands. She did not marry but did adopt three girls whom she loved as if she was their birth mother and each child became a grandmother and then great-grandmothers.

Each daughter passed on to their children the story of the dragon and the importance of displaying its image. Indeed even today in the 21st-century, archaeologists will sometimes still fine ancient jewellery and other artefacts with the image of the dragon upon them. Could this be in part because of the stories of long ago? Could it be that because of the old stories that suggested displaying the dragon's image would in fact ensure the real thing would forever sleep?

The centuries went by and with them the story changed. Some things were added and some things were changed but in essence the story remained the same until one day in mid - September the only living descendent of the eldest Princess was sitting under an oak tree and he was about to put down in words a story that had been handed down to him by his father years before.

It was a story that had been in his family for as long as anyone could remember. His name was Lucan and the year was 1014. He had with him a small box made of wood and metal and as much as he didn't know it he was about to make history.

Chapter 14
The Story of Iris

Morgana left South Wales two days after the departure of the four Princesses. Where she went or what she did for the next several hundred years is not known until suddenly her story picks up again as we travel to a different time in Britain and to a time when it had a different name and that was The United Kingdom of Great Britain and Ireland. The year is 1901 and a Queen Empress lays dying in a fine house on the Isle of Wight. She has been on the British throne for a very long time during which Great Britain had become the most powerful nation in the world, but the life of its constitutional head is now coming to an end and all of the country will grieve for her. Her children have married into the Royal houses of Europe and many of her descendants are now Kings and Queens in Europe and her name is remembered up and down the land from street names and public halls, even an entire era was named after her.

Queen Victoria wasn't always a little old woman. There was a time when she was a little girl and would play with her toys just like any other girl her age. She was a somewhat lonely child. Her father was dead and her suffocating mother kept her away from the outside world. Because of this she turned to other things such as making little dolls and reading, for she loved stories and had lots of books. Her nanny would read to her and when she became a little older she could read to herself and would do so for hours at a time.

There came a day when she was about ten years old, one of her tutors told her of a very old story that he had found in the archive of the British library in London. He told her that he would bring it to show her the following week. The little girl was intrigued and excited at the prospect of reading it.

During the week, however, the little girl become unwell with a slight cold and her mother ordered her to bed, and so on the morning her tutor arrived at Kensington Palace he was almost turned away but insisted on seeing the girl, promising to do nothing other than read her a story. To this her mother agreed. He went upstairs and into the girl's room along with one of the housemaids.

The young Princess Victoria was sat up in bed looking grumpy, not because she felt unwell but the fact that she felt fine and didn't want to be in bed all day. Greeting her he made himself comfortable in the chair next to the bed. The housemaid stood quietly next to the window. She was sent into the room too because it was deemed improper that a gentlemen of a lower class be alone in the bedroom of Princess Victoria. The tutor began telling the Princess Victoria about the story he had brought with him and the housemaids stood and listened too. She was a tall woman with long hair that was tied up and back under a housemaids white cap. She wore a long black gown with a white collar made of lace. Her eyes were the deepest blue. It was forbidden for the staff in the house to wear any kind of jewellery and so the housemaid wore her only ring around her neck on a chain and out of sight.

She simply adored the Princess Victoria and they were secret friends.

The tutor was explaining to the Princess that the story was written a very long time ago and it was a legend all about a prince and dragon, a treacherous King and a sorceress.

He had found the story by chance in the British library and that is where he was going to return it the following day.

It was in a small box made of wood and metal on top of a shelf. It was in at last three different forms of English and Welsh, however the tutor was a very clever man and had no trouble whatever in reading it, but he did write out the entire story on a separate piece of paper in red ink and in English just to make it a Little easier for himself.

His name was John Evans. He had studied at Oxford University but his family were from Wales. He was in his late twenties and unmarried. He lived in rooms in Kings Cross London.

He loved history and literature, and enjoyed the theatre and the countryside. His family was one of the oldest in South Wales and could trace their family line back over hundreds of years.

He was an extremely smart and well presented gentleman.

His cravat was neatly tied around his neck. The cravat pin that was used to keep it in place was rather unusual. It was a flat disc of bronze with a very small dragon engraved upon it.

He asked the Princess if she would like him to read it to her. She said yes at once because she too was a Princess and they were her favourite kind of stories. From his briefcase he brought out the box he had spoken of and carefully opened it and took out the papers, he then set them out on his lap and began to read...

"It came to pass that the Prince of South Wales and Uther Pendragon captured a dragon." By the end the little Princess was fascinated and asked if he would read it again and the obliging John Evans did just that. Although they both agreed it was a fascinating story it did not seem to have an ending but this of course did not take away from the fact that Princess Victoria and John Evans for that matter thought it was wonderful.

The housemaid stood quite still and all the time she was watching the expression on the little Princess's face. Then her eyes moved to John Evans and his cravat pin. Although her face showed no outward expression, on the inside she was overcome with emotion for she knew that a time was coming when this story would soon come to its final conclusion.

It may take another few hundred years to reach its outcome but to her that was no time at all!

The tutor went on to be knighted by Victoria. He also went on to write several books, one of which was called "The Dragon in the Snow" (his personal favourite).

He of course kept his own second copy of the dragon story but being a good and honest man he returned the little box and its original contents as well as his own written translation on a separate piece of paper in red ink to the British library where it would stay for the next 100 years or so.

As for the little Princess she never forgot that day and as she grew up the words of that story never left her. Eventually she married and went on to have nine children and in turn she told each of them the same story. Although some forgot it or didn't like it, her eldest son (whom she called Bertie) never forgot it and so when he had children of his own he too passed the story down to them and they did the same until one day many years later, a woman, indeed a Queen (whose husband was King George V) was sitting in a sun lit garden with her two eldest sons Edward and Albert, both of whom where young boys.

She too told them the very same story that her husband had once told her before they were married. Her eldest son simply laughed and ran off to climb a tree however Albert sat quietly and listened.

The years passed and her second son went on to be crowned King and emperor. He had two daughters named Elizabeth and Margaret. He was known to the world as His Majesty King George VI and so honouring a family tradition the day would come when he too told his daughters the same story that the tutor John Evans had told his great-great grandmother Victoria over 100 years before.

King George was a good man and he led the British people through the dark days of World War II. Both he and his wife would travel the country visiting hospitals and bomb sites. They became a symbol of determination to the people in the face of incredible odds. He had a great sense of pride in the Army, the Navy and the Air Force.

He also admired the members of the British secret service the men and woman that would enter occupied Europe to spy on and do all they could to bring down the Nazis and it was on the morning of May 1st 1946 at Buckingham Palace that the King was about to give a medal to a woman whose bravery went a long way in saving Britain form a new dark age.

Her name was Iris. She was sitting in a small room in the Palace. She arrived that morning with both her mother and father.

All three of them were nervous and excited for they were about to meet the King. Iris for her part did not really think that she deserved this great honour. She felt that anyone would do all they could to serve their country in any way they could, but the king and the rest of the country did not share her view for Iris was indeed a brave woman and now the time had come for her to be given the George Cross by the king himself.

Iris sat quietly next to her mother in the small room. Her father was looking out of the window into the inner courtyard of Buckingham Palace. They knew that at any moment the door would open and all three of them would be shown into the much bigger room next door where the King would be waiting for them.

Iris was thinking about what had brought her here to London today. Her mind began to go back just over four years to that dark night. There was no moon and a Lancaster bomber was flying over occupied Denmark. It had taken off some hours ago from an airbase in England. Inside there are four people, the pilot and co-pilot of the Royal Air Force and two British agents. The year is 1942 and World War II is raging across Europe. Its peoples are living in fear. The Nazis occupy most of Europe and Great Britain is threatened. They are travelling to a remote part of Denmark where one of them will make a parachute jump near the border with Germany.

Inside the plane the agents are discussing the mission. In theory it is very simple: locate a certain resistance cell and help equip and organise it to be more effective in Denmark's struggle for freedom. If the Nazis could be pushed out of Denmark then maybe other nations would follow and Nazi Germany would be defeated.

Only one agent is to carry out this mission. She is 21 years old. She has just finished intensive training at a secret base in Scotland and this is her first mission. She is brave and single-minded and dedicated to helping free Europe and in turn protecting her homeland of Great Britain from tyranny. Her code name is 'femina-draco' but her true name is Iris Owens.

Iris Jane Owens was born in the West Midlands where her family had lived for generations. She is an only child. Her parents owned and ran a butcher's shop in her home town and she attended the local grammar school.

She had an extremely normal upbringing and before the outbreak of war she was contented with her life. She would help out in the butcher's shop and she attended the local dance halls with her friends, but then on Sunday the 3rd of September 1939 when she was 18 years old she was in the sitting room of her home with her mother and father whilst the entire country was waiting impatiently for a radio broadcast from the Prime Minister Neville Chamberlain. It was due at 11 o'clock that morning, for Nazi Germany had invaded Poland and the country was waiting to hear what the British government's response was going to be.

Both her mother and father were worried and anxious, for they knew what war would bring. Her father had been a soldier and had seen action in Gallipoli in the Great War and her mother had been a nurse in a military hospital in France nursing wounded soldiers from the trenches.

As 11 o'clock approached her father switched on the wireless and then came the voice of the Prime Minister Mr Chamberlain:

"I am speaking to you from the cabinet room at 10 Downing Street. This morning, the British ambassador in Berlin handed the German government a final note, stating that if we hadn't heard from them by 11 o'clock and if they weren't prepared at once to withdraw their troops from Poland a state of war would exist between us. I have to tell you now that no such undertaking has been received, and that consequently this country is at war with Germany"

Her mother, whose name was Janice was the first to speak and looking out of the window she said "It's such a beautiful day fancy starting a war on such a beautiful day as this!" and then turning to her husband she said "We will have to prepare for the worst. I dare say there will be rationing and food shortages and prices will go up!"

Janice was a very practical woman and wasn't going to let any war affect her family's dinner table! Her father, whose name was Brian, nodded in agreement, looked at Iris and said "My dear, there are difficult times ahead. This war is going to be long and costly in every respect. I never thought to see another war in my life time!"

The three of them sat in silence for a while, they knew only too well that their lives were going to change in the months and indeed years to come.

Over the next few months, Brian built a small air raid shelter in the back garden and Janice sacrificed her beautiful flower beds to make way for growing vegetables. Just like all their neighbours, they observed the blackout rules at night and the family began to ration its customers in the butcher's shop in accordance with the Ministry of Food rules.

It is said that bad news always comes in threes. Six months had passed since Neville Chamberlain had delivered his speech on that beautiful day at the beginning of September and there was a new Prime Minister and the country was well and truly at war.

In Iris's hometown, great numbers of young men had signed up to join the military and then one Thursday morning in March a boy on a bicycle was delivering a telegram to a house just three doors down from where the More family lived. Within minutes the muffled sobbing of Mrs More could be heard from the house.

Later Iris heard that Richard, a young man her own age whom she had known all her life, had been killed in action somewhere in Egypt! This devastating news wasn't the first or indeed the last that day because only an hour before, her married older sister had telephoned to say that her brother-in-law's spitfire had been shot down over the English Channel and he was missing, presumed dead.

Iris had just returned from the butcher's shop on the high street. She had been to tell her father the news of their neighbour's son and of her sister's brother-in-law. Her mother Janice was at home and Iris was intending to make lunch for the two of them.

As she opened the front door her mother came running down the hall way holding a newspaper and to say that there had been an air raid over London last night that had killed over 50 people, including children! At this news Iris froze with a feeling of immense anger and sorrow. There came over her a feeling that only ever happens to someone once or twice in their lifetime a feeling of blind determination and at that very moment she made up her mind that she must act! She must do something to help stop this devastation!

She must do her bit and join the fight against Nazi Germany. Kissing her mother and running out of the house, she made her way back to the high street and to the recruiting office. She burst through the door where she was met by a man in military dress sitting at a desk, a pen in one hand and a smoking pipe in the other. He looked up at her with surprise and said "Good day to you miss.

What can I do for you?"

He had a kind face and Iris explained that she wanted, indeed she needed, to do something to assist in the war effort.

She told him that she was desperate to help serve the country she loved so much. She told him that she was a crack shot with a rifle because when she was a teenager her grandfather taught her how to use a rifle safely and professionally when in the school holidays she would go and stay with him and her grandma on their farm in the country. She went on to tell him that she could speak German because when she was in school she would attend 'language club' after school hours where she learnt not only how to speak German but also how to write it.

The soldier could see that Iris was entirely serious in what she was saying. Smiling he stood up and said "My name is Sergeant Montgomery Davis of his Majesty's Royal Welsh Fusiliers" holding out his hand he added "But you can call me Monty."

After they shook hands he invited her to sit down and explained that he was there to help recruit men in to the British Army, but she wasn't the first woman to come in looking for advice on how to serve their country and he would be happy to help.

They talked for several minutes about the kind of service that was open to women in war time, most of which included working in factories or in the auxiliary services such as air-raid wardens, fire officers and evacuation officers. There were also opportunities in becoming a land girl or indeed a nurse like her mother was in World War One.

Iris felt extremely enthusiastic about becoming an air-raid warden and asked Monty were she could go to sign up. She thought this would be something appropriate, not only supporting her country but also her community and for the most part it would be at night and she would have time to help her mother around the house and her father in the shop in the day time.

Monty did not speak or answer the question. He simply said "Miss Owens, I think your particular skills could be put too much better use in the service of your country. Indeed you can use a rifle and converse in German, and those abilities could be very useful indeed. Now I cannot promise anything, however, I would like you to meet my superior officer and he would be able to advise you much better than I on the options that may be available to you. If it is convenient to you I would like you to return here in one hour and I would like, if I may, to introduce you to Major Peters. You will find him a friendly agreeable kind of chap. I suggest you have a cup of tea in the Victorian tea room around the corner and return in one hour."

Iris, feeling somewhat excited at meeting the Major and hearing what he would have to say, thanked Monty and left the Recruitment office. She crossed the street, turned the corner and entered the teashop. After ordering a pot of tea for one she took a table by the window. It started to rain. Iris was watching some soldiers with their sweethearts walking very quickly up the High Street towards the Picture Palace.

Iris was imagining the Major to be tall and distinguished. She worried about how she would address him? What was it he was going to say? She poured herself a second cup of tea and checked her watch, as she did not want to be late on getting back to the recruiting office to meet the Major.

The bell above the door tinkled as the door of the tearoom opened. Iris didn't pay any attention to the middle-aged, somewhat overweight man that came in wearing a black raincoat and hat. He was holding a roll umbrella. The man went to the counter and ordered himself a pot of tea and a Welsh cake. Taking off his hat he looked around the tea room. There were around seven customers including Iris and several empty tables but the man walked over to the table where Iris was sitting. He coughed politely. Iris looked up and he said, "Excuse me Miss, is this seat taken? May I join you?"

Iris felt confused because there were at least five empty tables where he could sit alone. She didn't know what to say at first and then remembering her manners she said "Yes, of course." The man thanked her and sat down. Iris was feeling a little uncomfortable and was about to make her excuses and leave.

She would just have to be a little early at the recruitment office, for she wasn't used to strangers sitting right next to her in tea rooms. She was about to stand up when the man spoke. "My Dear, please let me introduce myself. My name is Major Peters and you must be Miss Owens, am I right?"

Nodding, Iris said "Yes, Yes I am." She looked surprised! Why was the Major here in the tearoom?

Before she could ask him or say anything the waitress came to the table with the pot of tea that the Major had ordered along with the Welsh cake. After she had gone back to the counter, the major spoke first in a whisper "Miss Owens, please let me explain. First of all, please accept my apologies for I am not in the habit of distressing young ladies in tearooms. As I said my name is Major Peters and like Sergeant Davis I work in the recruitment office." By now Iris was feeling somewhat calmer and thought maybe Monty had made some kind of mistake. Maybe he thought Iris did indeed arrange to meet the Major in the tearoom. As if he was reading her mind, he went on and said "I know of course that you were asked to return to the recruiting office to meet with me, however, because of the circumstances I thought it prudent to meet here instead."

Iris was again confused; she was only interested in joining the ARP. Looking at him she said "What kind of circumstances are you referring to Sir?" Smiling and picking up the Welsh cake he began to eat.

Iris was feeling incredibly confused and she had a lot of questions but did not wish to ask them until he had finished eating. The Major, who had by now finished his Welsh Cake, looked Iris straight in the eye and said "As I'm sure you will understand there are no end of fine young men who can fire a gun and/or speak German in this country, however finding ladies who can do such things is more or less impossible. So when the good sergeant told me of your abilities I knew at once that I wanted to meet and talk with you. I also felt it would be better for all kinds or reasons to meet with you here."

Iris too thought that the fact she could speak German would be useful in dealing with refugees or maybe as an interpreter for prisoners of war and that is why she had mentioned it to Monty in the recruitment office.

"Miss Owens," he continued "I will now be blunt and to the point. The government department to which I belong is tasked with recruiting special agents to, in some cases, travel abroad to occupied Europe and carry out missions to thwart the enemy. Before I continue I must tell you that the enemy don't like what we are doing and their treatment of anybody who is caught is quite....."

Iris by now was in total shock and interrupting the Major she said, "And you want me to be one of those agents you speak of? You want me to be some kind of spy?"

"In a word, yes" said the Major. His facial expression did not change and he went on, "The enemy is close. The Nazis are just across the English Channel and they want this island.

Indeed they do and they will not stop until the swastika is flying over the Palace of Westminster. Now I understand that you are surprised by everything I have said but you must think about what it is I am asking of you." Taking a fountain pen and a piece of paper from the inside of his jacket he asked Iris to write down her address and said "I will call to see you at home the day after tomorrow and we will discuss this matter further. Please do not make any decision right now. I will bring with me a female officer who will be under the guise of a recruitment officer should anyone ask." Iris did not speak she simply wrote down her address and nodded in agreement.

"I have one last thing to say before I wish you a good afternoon" said the Major "And that is under no circumstances whatsoever can you tell anyone of what we have spoken about today, can I please have your solemn promise you will not divulge anything to anyone?"

Iris looked the major straight in the eye and said "Sir, you have my solemn promise."

The Major smiled and said, "Very well then, until the day after tomorrow. Would 10 o'clock be convenient?" "Yes, major that's convenient" said Iris and they both stood up and the major shook hands with Iris and left the tearoom.

That night as Iris was lying in bed trying to sleep her mind was working overtime. All she could think about was 'The Meeting' she had had that day with the Major. There were so many questions running around in her mind!

She fell in to a dreamless sleep, the kind of sleep that when you wake only feels like you have only been sleeping for five minutes when it fact it's been hours.

When she woke up to a wet Sunday morning, Iris was no closer to making up her mind but she knew that she had 24 hours to do so. She told herself that she would have to make up her mind by the time she went back to bed that night. Could she do this, become a spy? She washed, dressed and went down to breakfast. Both her father and mother joined her at the table because her father didn't open the shop on a Sunday.

Brian was reading the newspaper as Iris walked in to the kitchen. On the front page were the headlines: "Britain Victorious In Atlantic." The newspapers were always filled with good news and British victories, but Iris, like most people, didn't always believe it all because men were still dying and there was no end in sight.

The day seemed to go by very quickly and before Iris knew where the time had gone, it was again time for bed. She had told both her mother and father that two people would be calling to the house the next day to give her some information about becoming an air-raid warden. She did not think there was any problem with this and she was sure that the Major would understand. Both her parents agreed that it was a good idea, although her father seemed worried but did not say anything to discourage his daughter.

As Iris went up to bed she knew that the time had come to make up her mind and to make the decision, a decision that could very well effect the rest of her life, indeed it could even take her life. As she lay down on her bed her eyes began to close. It was warm and quiet in her bedroom, her bed was soft and she began to drift off to sleep.

It was coming up to 10 o'clock in the morning and Iris was sitting in the living room. She knew that at any moment the doorbell would ring and her life would change.

Both her mother and father were not at home. They had both left that morning to open the shop and so Iris went to open the door to two people: a man and a woman. The man was Major Peters whom she had met just days before in what was a somewhat strange encounter in a tearoom.

He was dressed in the same black raincoat and hat that he was wearing the day they met. The woman, who was in a smart uniform, had the bluest eyes Iris had ever seen. Her hair was long but tied up and back.

Iris asked them both in and showed them in to the living room and asked them both to sit down. Major Peters introduced the woman as Lance Corporal Jones.

They spent some time making small talk until Major Peters said, "My dear lady, as you know we have come here today to ask you formally if you would like to enrol into the service which we represent, but please remember what I said to you the other day and what is and could be involved." Iris did not say a word and the Major continued "If you wish to do so then you should know that you will have to leave this house and this town and travel north to Scotland just as soon as the arrangements can be made to undertake an intensive training regime. You see, no matter what you may read in the newspapers this war isn't going well for us at all and we must act quickly."

Up until now Lance Corporal Jones had said very little. She was looking at Iris with what seemed to be a great deal of interest and said, "Miss Owens, could you please tell us a little about yourself and your family. I ask this as I always feel that it is important to find out as much as possible about anyone who wishes to join the department." Iris told them both that up until now she lived a rather simple life and that she never did anything unusual or indeed heroic, but now that her home was threatened she was ready to do what she could to help. Lance Corporal Jones smiled and asked Iris about her parents and her family history. Iris, supposing that this was for security reasons, told them that her family came from Wales some 150 years ago and it was her great-grandparents on her father's side that had first opened the butcher's shop in the town that now belonged to her father and mother.

She told them both that her ancestors were once Welsh royalty, and as she said this she giggled and told them that she never believed such nonsense and it was her father that was interested in such things.

Indeed he had an extensive family tree all written out on a big piece of paper and sometimes he would bring it out and they would all discuss it as a family but it went back so far that neither Iris or her mother could understand how anyone could ever know such things from so long ago, but her father was adamant that it was correct because he had put many years of work and study in to it.

Lance Corporal Jones seemed to be very interested in what Iris had to say, but the Major wanted to move on and talk about why they were there that morning. Looking at Iris he said "My dear lady I will have to be going soon but before I do, I would like, if I may, to have your decision and then I will leave you and Lance Corporal Jones to talk it over." Iris got to her feet, as did the Major, and talking his hand and shaking it Iris said "Yes Major, I have made my decision and I would like to do my bit for my King and for my country." The major was a little taken aback by this formal announcement but smiling he said "Good for you, good for you! I will leave you now and Lance Corporal Jones will fill you in with all the information you need. Please sit down, Miss Owens, I will find my own way to the front door and shaking her hand again he smiled and left the room then moments later Iris and Lance Corporal Jones heard the front door open and close.

The two women were now alone together in the living room. For a moment Iris didn't know what to say and simply smiled and asked if she would like a cup of tea but Lance Corporal Jones just smiled and said, "Miss Owens, could I have a look at the family tree you spoke of?

I find it very interesting and if you would be so kind as to let me see it I would be very grateful indeed." Iris could not understand why this woman wanted to see her family tree but deciding not to question it she went to the sideboard, opened the top drawer and brought out a roll of paper and, removing the potted plant from the coffee table, she unrolled it so they could both see it. It was very detailed and the writing was very small but at the top was the name Quintus Antistius and then there was a small vertical line and the name Aoife was written and then it went on and on, there were over 500 names, some of the names were very unusual, some had a date next to them but a lot did not and at the very bottom was written the name Iris Owens.

Lance Corporal Jones began to run her finger from the top of the family tree and then followed the line from what was not a person's name but just the words "Fourth Princess." This particular line ended with Iris.

Lance Corporal Jones did not say anything about it at all and just thanked Iris for showing it to her. She then strangely and abruptly completely changed the subject and went on to tell Iris that in the coming days she would reserve notification by post from the Ministry of Defence informing her to report to a certain place in Scotland where she would be trained and receive further information about her new role.

Sitting back in the armchair, Lance Corporal Jones reached into her military issue handbag and brought out a small box made from wood and metal and placed it on the coffee table. At once Iris' eyes were fixed upon it. It looked ancient and Iris could not resist asking what it was, but Lance Corporal Jones did not answer straight away and said, "Miss Owens, as you can imagine, we at the department you wish to join are secretive in nature and again, as you can imagine, we expect our agents to be of the very best quality and as such from time to time we ask that they carry out what they may consider to be unusual tasks and I am going to ask just that of you right now. Within this box there are two pieces of paper. Written upon them is a story.

They are identical stories, the only difference is one is written in modern English and the other is written in both ancient Welsh and English.

I have the distinct impression you have heard this story before only the ending is missing from both stories and I would like you to please finish it for me right now."

She then opened the box, took out the two pieces of paper and laid them on the coffee table in front of Iris. At once Iris could see that one was very old indeed and written in more than one hand and in different languages. The other was written in red ink and Iris had no trouble whatsoever in reading and understanding it. To her astonishment it was the story of the dragon. She of course knew this story but she always thought it to be a family story, a story handed down through her family and not known by any one else.

She never had any idea that anyone else outside her family knew of it. It was a child's story that her father had told her at bed time when she was a little girl, but to Iris the most puzzling thing was why this was happening in the first place. What did this story have to do with her joining the British Secret Service if that indeed was the true name of the department Lance Corporal Jones was referring to? The only conclusion that Iris could come to was that it was some kind of test or initiation. She decided not to question it and so picking up the piece of paper with the words written in red ink she began to read.

It came to pass that the Prince of South Wales and Uther Pendragon forced an enormous dragon into

a great pit on Caerphilly Mountain in South Wales. But Uther betrayed the Prince, and he was killed in a great battle defending the Welsh people from the marauding Anglo-Saxons.

Uther never told anyone exactly where the Dragon was imprisoned and took the secret with him to his grave.

Before he too was killed he asked the witch Morgana to put a spell on the mountain so that the dragon would never be discovered but dragons can live forever. Many people have dedicated their lives searching for it over the last 1000 years but no one has been able to find it and many have gone mad in its pursuit

"The centuries will pass and the people will say that they can hear the dragon roaring deep inside the Mountain!"

Take heed! For when Morgana's spell is all but ended and when the old ways of Magic are completely forgotten by the Welsh people, the dragon will break free of the mountain and take its revenge on all Britain"

When she'd finished she looked up from the paper at Lance Corporal Jones and said "I was told this story by my father when I was a little girl and although some of the details are a little different it is more or less the same, how do you know that story Corporal?" But Lance Corporal Jones did not answer her question. Instead she put her hand in to her bag and brought out two fountain pens and a silver ring that had an unusual white stone upon it.

She placed the ring on to the second finger of her right hand and then handing one pen to Iris she asked her to complete the last verse of the story. Iris by now was incredibly confused. Why did this woman suddenly put a ring on her finger? Iris decided not to question this slightly strange behaviour because she didn't know exactly how to word the question. Instead she simply picked up the pen, unscrewed the lid, and began to write. The ink was the same colour red as the rest of the writing on the page. Iris wrote the following words.

The only hope there ever was for Wales was that the dragon would forever sleep within the mountain and the only way this could happen was to display its image right across Wales. Only then would the dragon forever sleep.

To Iris that was the end of the story as far as she remembered it and to her it was just a childish fairytale of no consequence. Looking over to Lance Corporal Jones she noticed that she too was writing but in black ink and on the other much older piece of paper but the words were exactly the same as her own.

Lance Corporal Jones then took both pieces of paper, put them both back into the strange little box and placed it carefully into her handbag.

She then thanked Iris and reminded her that the Ministry of Defence would be writing to her and with that she said good bye and left a very confused Iris standing alone in the living room.

Lance Corporal Jones and Iris never met again and Iris never forgot the strange encounter.

As the days passed and Iris went over the visit from the Major and the Lance Corporal in her mind there were so many questions, but soon enough the letter she had been expecting finally arrived from the Ministry of Defence and before she knew it she was in Scotland training extremely hard both physically and mentally for the tasks to come.

Her mission in Nazi-occupied Denmark was extremely successful, and because of this she was just moments away from meeting his Majesty King George VI and to receive the George Cross for courage.

Chapter 15
Princess Elizabeth

George VI was a man loved by his people and by his family. He too loved Great Britain, his wife and his daughters very much and regretted deeply the fact that he could not spend as much time with them as he wished, but one night when his youngest daughter Margaret was asleep and his eldest daughter Elizabeth was almost asleep, he and his wife crept into their bedroom.

It was Christmas Eve and they wanted to lay out some presents for their daughters.

Quietly they entered, and George suddenly felt as if he wanted to tell his daughter a bedtime story. He could count on one hand the amount of times he had ever had the opportunity to do so, and so sitting down on Elizabeth's bed he began to tell her a story that his mother had told him when he was little.

Elizabeth was nine years old that year and in George's opinion old enough to hear a story about a dragon in a mountain in South Wales and as his wife, who was also called Elizabeth, laid out some presents at the bottom of each of their daughters beds he began.

"It came to pass that the Prince of South Wales and Uther Pen dragon captured a dragon…"

When he had finished Elizabeth, who was only half awake, simply said, "Thank you Papa and Happy Christmas."

As the King and Queen quietly left the room, they made their way to their own sitting room. Sitting down next to the fire the Queen turned to her husband and said "I enjoyed your story, but somehow it seemed unfinished?" The King smiled and said "Yes, I always thought that too but isn't that the best kind of story? For a story with no ending can't have an unhappy ending."

The years passed, the war came and went and the King saw his two little girls grow up and become fine young ladies, but the story of his eldest daughter had only just began.

The year is 1947 and it's time to leave Great Britain and travel to Cape Town, South Africa. A young woman is celebrating her 21st birthday and is about to make a radio broadcast. The speech she is about to deliver will contain a promise, a promise of dedication and service, a promise that she will never break.

Her name is Her Royal Highness Princess Elizabeth Alexandra Mary Windsor and she is destined to be one of the greatest monarchs of all time, but today she is just 21 years old and is about to dedicate herself to millions of people all over the world, and she does so with grace and sincerity.

She is staying in the house of the governor of South Africa and that afternoon, after the broadcast, she was trying to rest on her bed, partly because of the heat and partly because she was very excited as that evening there is to be a grand ball to celebrate her birthday.

She could not sleep. Instead she decided to take a walk in the gardens. As she walked under the trees all she could think about was her beautiful ball gown her father had bought for her. Suddenly out of the corner of her eye she sees a lady sitting on a stone bench. She was quite alone. She was wearing a stylish hat and a modern trouser suit, her hair was in a modern style under her hat and her eyes were a deep blue. She wasn't wearing any jewellery except for a silver ring with an unusual white stone that didn't seem to match her up-to-the-minute fashionable look. She looked rather out of place and Elizabeth could not take her eyes off her. She seemed quite alone and looked somewhat melancholy in the hot African afternoon sun.

Elizabeth, being an incredibly inquisitive young woman, slowly walked up to her. She coughed quietly and politely and the lady looked up. She didn't seem at all surprised in fact her expression suggested that she knew she would be meeting someone in the garden that afternoon. Looking up at Elizabeth she began to smile. Her eyes were bright blue and her face was beaming with delight. Standing up and curtsying she said, "You are the Princess Elizabeth. I am indeed incredibly pleased to meet you. Will you not sit with me for a little while?" Elizabeth was intrigued by this lady. Although she didn't recognise her, she felt as though they had met before. Deciding that she was probably mistaken she sat down and the lady then sat down next to her. Neither of them spoke for a time until Elizabeth said, "Are you enjoying the gardens ma'am?"

The lady nodded but she did not speak. Instead she just looked at Elizabeth and, smiling, she reached behind her and brought out a small handbag. It was pale blue with a silver clasp with brown edging. Without a word she opened it and took out a small box. It looked incredibly old and aged with time. Elizabeth's eyes were fixed open it and her curiosity got the better of her and she said "What a strange little box you have there, ma'am. Could it be that you keep something precious in it?"

The box was made of wood and metal and looked handmade. Elizabeth could not tell what kind of wood it was, but before she could ask the lady looked at her and said "My dear, this box is from the British Library in London, where it has been ignored for over one hundred years and it was borrowed from there and then placed back there by a man who truly understood its importance and by happy coincidence it has now come in to my personal possession and I would like to tell you dear princess of how this came to be so there is no confusion surrounding its ownership. I myself lived in London before the war and worked as a junior member of staff in the British Library.

I spent my days sorting through different papers and manuscripts, and each day it would be the same until the day came when the supervisor of the department in which I worked came to my desk as usual with a great pile of dusty papers for me to sort through. On top of the pile was this very box. My supervisor was an unimaginative, narrow minded man who simply told me that he had looked though the box and inside was just some bits of paper one of which was written a childish story and the other was written mostly in a language he could not understand, and that it had no place in the British library and would I please dispose of it. I of course did not throw it away as he suggested. I kept it for myself and here it is." The lady touched the top with her hand, smiled, looked at Elizabeth and said "Today you made a promise to dedicate your life not only to the people of the country of your birth but to countless millions all over the world. That promise I am sure will echo through the years and into the next century. The words *'I swear before you all that my whole life, be it long or short will be dedicated to your service'* will never be forgotten by those who choose to remember it, and I'm sure that you will always remember the importance of a solemn promise."

As she said it the lady looked down at the ring on her finger and continued "My dear, one day you will become a great queen, I am sure of it, and like so many queens and kings before you, you will have it in your power to do great things or terrible things. It will be up to you to decide what you will do with the great responsibility you will hold but I am sure you will be a fine monarch.

Yes you will have plenty of men and women that will advise and guide you and of course act in your name. Some will be genuine and some will not and it will be up to you to act in accordance with your wisdom and of course your conscience."

Elizabeth sat quietly listening. She was somewhat mesmerised by what this lady (who for some reason or other she felt she knew but could not remember ever meeting) was saying to her.

The ladies words felt like a river flowing over her. She did not know how to respond to everything she had just heard and all she could say was "Thank you, ma'am. I will of course endeavour to always do the right thing when I am Queen"

To this the lady smiled and patted Elizabeth's hand, which again surprised Elizabeth a great deal. She was brought up with a strict understanding of protocol, but for some reason none of that seemed to matter at that moment, and the fact that a stranger was talking to her, and even patted her hand, seemed the most normal and natural thing in the world at that precise moment on a bench under a tree in the grounds of a fine house in the middle of South Africa.

The conversation then turned to the weather. It's something that most of us turn to when there is nothing more to say, but in this case there was one more thing to talk about and that was the little box that was now sitting on the lady's lap, almost forgotten.

Without a word the lady stood up holding the box and said "Dear Elizabeth, this is for you. Inside you will find a story. All I ask is that you read it. To you it will be unbelievable but every word is true. It is an old story with many authors and although it may seem like a legend to you, please remember that with a lot of legends some facts have been added and some facts taken away but the essence of the story is true.

"It has taken over a thousand years to write but its history goes back to a time before time. The history of your people, your ancestors and the land of your birth is intertwined with in it.

"It has been carefully preserved and protected for centuries, and now it is time to be acted upon. Take heed, my dear Princess, and do not ignore my words or the story with in this box, for it is as relevant today as it was on the day the first person wrote the first line."

She then handed the box to Elizabeth and said "Happy Birthday."

We will meet again one day I am sure, but until then I ask only one thing from you and that is when you become Queen you act on what is written on the paper within this box, will you promise to do so?"

Elizabeth took the box from the lady and by now was quite overwhelmed by all of this. Who was this strange woman whom she thought was familiar to her?

Why was she telling her all of this here in a garden? What on Earth was in this box? Elizabeth was about to ask these questions when suddenly she heard a voice calling to her from across the neatly kept lawn. She turned and saw her mother walking very quickly towards her. Turning back to the lady she said without thinking, but remembering the paramount importance of a promise, "When I am Queen and when the time is right, I promise that I will act on what is written on the paper in this box. Thank you for my birthday present."

The lady stood up, curtsied and picked up her handbag. At that moment, Elizabeth's mother walked up to them. Again the lady curtsied saying "Good afternoon Your Majesty." (Elizabeth's mother was indeed a Queen being the wife of George VI) Queen Elizabeth smiled at the lady with an air of suspicion. She too partly recognised her but did not say so. There was a moment's silence and the lady said, "Please excuse me, your Majesty." Curtsying for the last time, she said, "I must take my leave now." Queen Elizabeth smiled and said "Of course, madam" and without another word the lady walked backwards four or five steps and just before she turned she made brief eye contact with Princess Elizabeth and walked away towards the gates.

When the lady was out of ear shot Queen Elizabeth turned to her daughter and asked her who the lady was, and why she didn't introduce her. Elizabeth explained that she was a well wisher that wanted to give her a small birthday present. Queen Elizabeth looked at the box and was not very impressed, for to her it just seemed like a battered piece of tat.

Elizabeth didn't tell her mother anything about the conversation they had had. Instead the conversation moved from the lady to that evening's celebrations.

Elizabeth returned to her room after the ball that had been a tremendous success. It was around 4 o'clock in the morning by the time she was quite alone. All her servants had left her at last and she was sitting at her dressing table, having taken the small box of wood and metal out of the drawer and placed it on the marble tabletop.

She was feeling nervous and part of her didn't want to open the box. Her encounter earlier that afternoon before in the garden left her feeling excited to open the box but now she felt apprehensive because of the promise she had made to the lady that had given it to her only hours ago. She had promised to act on whatever is written on the paper in the box, but what if it was something terrible? What if it was something ridiculous or impossible?

She closed her eyes and sat back in her chair. There was total silence. As she slowly opened her eyes she was looking at a framed black-and-white photograph that she had brought with her from London to remind her of home. She liked to put photographs around the room where she happened to be staying as it would help stop her feeling home sick.

It was a photograph of her and her grandmother Queen Mary on Elizabeth's 10th Birthday that she had celebrated with her family. She smiled and remembered that day very well. As she stared at the picture a strange feeling came over her.

She had seen the photograph countless times of course, but now and for what felt like the first time, she began to notice the people in the background. There were four of them: one was her little sister Margaret, who wasn't looking at the camera; the second was one of her mother's brothers; the third was a man she didn't recognise and the last was a lady. She was holding a silver tray of canapés and was looking directly into the camera with no expression what so ever. She looked to be a servant. She was standing about five feet behind her and Queen Mary, and Elizabeth knew at once who she was. She knew but could hardly believe that this lady in the photograph was the same lady she had met in the garden the afternoon before.

Although the photograph was black and white the eyes of the lady seemed to shine out of the photograph. Elizabeth was in a state of semi-shock, and although the two ladies were dressed extremely differently they were identical!

But how could this be? How could a lady, indeed a servant, from 11 years ago in London be the same woman whom she had had a 20 minute Conversation with on a bench in Cape Town?

As far as Elizabeth could tell the woman in question hadn't aged a day! Elizabeth knew what she had to do next. With both hands she picked up the box and opened it.

The two small hinges were rusted and it was a little difficult to lift the lid. Inside was a tightly folded piece of incredibly old paper.

Elizabeth knew of course that there was paper inside the box as the lady on the bench had told her so. Looking at it Elizabeth at once gently removed it from the box and unfolded it. It looked extremely old and some of the writing was faded with time. There was what looked like four separate entries written on the paper. The last was the easiest to read and her eyes naturally fell upon those particular words, and the Princess read a story of a dragon that was asleep inside a Mountain! She had heard of Caerphilly Mountain, she knew that it was in Wales and not far from Cardiff and she was sure that she had heard this story before! Looking in to the mirror of her dressing table she tried very hard to remember when she had heard it and who had told her but try as she did she could not remember it. She told herself that in the morning she would ask the one person she trusted more than any other and that was her father King George VI, for she knew that he would listen and not judge.

However she would not tell him the full story about the lady on the bench, only ask if he knew anything about a story that involved South Wales, a Mountain or a dragon.

She, of course, knew who Morgana was, she was the witch who played a part in the Arthurian legends and everyone in Britain and probably South Africa for that matter knew her name but it was only legend wasn't it?

All of the stories of King Arthur and his magic sword, of Merlin and Camelot were just stories?

She tried to put all of that to the back of her mind and again picked up the two pieces of paper. The first was almost impossible to read (except for the last paragraph) as the writing was faded and in a language she did not understand, although further down the page she did pick out certain words such as Caerphilly and again the name Morgana, but the rest was in ancient Welsh and a form of extremely old English that she could not read.

Putting the first piece of paper aside for a moment, she picked up the second and to her joy and excitement she noticed that it was all written in modern English. Each paragraph was set out exactly the same as it was on the first sheet of paper and in red ink, only the last verse although written in modern English and in red ink it was definitely written by a different person.

Her eyes were fixed upon it and she began to read…..

By the time she had finished the story she was in a state of shock! She didn't know what to do or think.

She also knew now for sure that she had been told this story before but a very long time ago although she could not remember the ending at all. It was probably her father who told her when she was a little girl! Feeling excited but very tired she thought it best to go to bed, it was now almost 5 o'clock in the morning and she was exhausted, and so taking another brief look at the photograph and the lady from her 10th Birthday she retired to bed feeling determined that later that day she would speak to her father about this extraordinary story.

Princess Elizabeth fell in to a deep sleep and didn't wake until midday. Her mother decided to leave her wake up in her own time for it had been an extremely late night.

The South African sun was shining brightly when the Princess eventually awoke and for a moment she did not remember anything from the night before.

Then came a knock at the door and in came her lady's maid. Sitting up in bed Elizabeth suddenly remembered everything and did not want to waste any time in speaking to her father!

She dressed quickly with the assistance of her maid and rushed downstairs. She knew that her father would be in the sitting room at this time listening to the BBC World Service on the wireless for he liked to keep up to date with what was going on at home in Britain.

She did not rush in to the room for she did not want to alarm her father in any way.

She had a lot of questions regarding the strange and somewhat troubling story she had read the night before.

Standing outside the door to the sitting room she took a deep breath and decided she would not mention the lady she had met yesterday or the strange little box that she just wanted to know if her father knew of the story and if so had he maybe told her and of course and most importantly where he had heard it and when.

Opening the door to the rather old-fashioned room, filled with Victorian furniture and paintings of different scenes and areas of South Africa, the first thing that caught her eye was an incredibly large painting of her father, dressed in his Royal robes and crown that was hanging over the fireplace here in the sitting room in the home of the governor of South Africa, for just like her grandfather and great-grandfather he was the constitutional king of South Africa.

She was used to seeing such things and never really thought much about it because she knew who she was and the family she was born in too.

There, in an ancient looking armchair sat her father, eyes closed and listening to the wireless. It was a news story about how Britain was facing one of its coldest winters in living memory. The reporter was talking about freezing conditions and lack of coal. She knew that her father never wanted to leave Britain, preferring instead to stay with his people as he had done in World War II.

As she walked further into the room the King opened his eyes and he greeted her in his usual cheerful way. She sat next to him in another ancient armchair.

They talked for some time about the ball the night before and the broadcast she had made.

Elizabeth then began to steer the conversation to her childhood and old stories, stories that maybe he had told her when she was small. They talked and laughed about the stories he would make up for her and her sister Margaret when they were little girls. Elizabeth asked her father if he knew of any stories that told of a dragon in South Wales. Smiling he said of course he did. There was one story in particular that he was told when he was a boy. "Don't you remember me telling you the tale of the dragon that is inside the mountain near Cardiff?" said the King. "Surely you must remember it, I told you one Christmas Eve when you were a little girl."

Elizabeth suddenly became hot and nervous. Looking at her father she said "No, Papa, I have no memory of that at all, please tell me it again."

The palms of Elizabeth's hands became damp and she felt incredibly nervous. The King smiled and told his daughter to press the call bell for tea and he would again tell her the story.

The King loved spending time with his daughter in this way, for he knew that very soon the time would come when she would marry and he would probably see less of her.

Within 10 minutes a servants came with a tray of tea and cakes and they both helped themselves.

Sitting back in her armchair with her tea, she listened as the king began to tell the story, a story that would change the future Queen's life forever.

Finishing his cake the King was smiling and looking over to his daughter as began to tell the story...

"It came to pass that a Prince of South Wales and Uther Pendragon captured a dragon and..."

He went on and told the story that was more or less the same version that was written on the piece of paper that was in the little box that was at that moment in the drawer of Princess Elizabeth's dressing table.

The King did not however include the last verse but Elizabeth knew of course what it was for it was written on two pieces of paper that was at this very moment in a small box in her dressing table.

Smiling, the King then helped himself to another cup of tea and a cake. Looking up from his tea, the King noticed his daughter was just staring into space. "Are you feeling quite well, Elizabeth?" asked the King. She was in a complete state of shock. She could not move or speak. Her father had just told her a story that he was told as a boy and it matched almost word for word to what was written on the piece of paper in the old box.

She could not understand how this could be! Also there was the lady in the garden to consider.

Why did she give her the box and how on earth could the servant in the photograph in her room be the same lady in the garden the day before? However strange that particular part of the mystery was, Elizabeth was sure they were the same person. If nothing else she was absolutely sure of that fact.

She didn't want to tell her father anything at this point and so pulling herself together she asked him if he could remember when he had told her this remarkable story. He of course could remember the exact date, for it was Christmas Eve when she was nine years old. As he was explaining the fact that he and her mother had come in to her and her sister Margaret's bedroom, Elizabeth began to remember. She began to remember her father sitting on the end of her bed and telling her this great story. Feeling even more excited she said "Papa, where did you hear that story? Who told you?" Slightly smiling at his daughter's excitement, he explained that his mother told him when he too was aged about nine years old.

The royal visit to South Africa came to an end, and it was time to return to England. The sea voyage was long and when they arrived at the dock Queen Mary (Elizabeth's grandmother) was there to welcome them home.

Elizabeth was pleased to be home too and had two things on her mind and that was to visit Wales and specifically the town of Caerphilly and to find out who the lady in the photograph was, and if indeed she was the same lady from South Africa whom she had met that hot afternoon on her 21st birthday.

Elizabeth made up her mind that a visit to Wales was the more important of the two, for she felt that her visit would answer a lot of her questions. It needed great deal of planning, not to mention a great deal of secrecy, for she was one of the most important people in the land for one day she would be Queen, and it was not fitting that she be seen travailing to a small City with just one companion.

In this case the companion was her most trusted Lady in Waiting, her name was Cherie and she was a loyal and trusted friend and Elizabeth trusted her completely. However, she found it prudent not to tell Cherie, why she wished to visit South Wales, after all it was an outlandish tale of dragons and child-like legends. She simply told her that she wanted to have a weekend away alone in Wales and not be expected to open a town hall or give a speech. In short she wished to be incognito for the duration of her stay. Of course a lot of preparations had to be made; Elizabeth did not wish to attract any attention. There would be no jewels or fancy clothes, she would dress modestly and organised for them both to stay in a small modest hotel in Cardiff. They would rent a car, which Elizabeth would drive herself.

Elizabeth told her father and mother that she was going to visit friends and because this was not unusual there were no difficult or awkward questions to answer.

Two second class train tickets were booked and the day came at last for the both of them to visit South Wales. Elizabeth did not have much of a plan of what to do when she got there.

She knew after looking at maps that Caerphilly was around ten miles from the centre of Cardiff; she also knew there was a ruined castle in the middle of the town that was built around 1275 by the 7th Earl of Gloucester.

The train arrived in Cardiff on time and the two companions made their way to the hotel. They had a room each next to each other and that evening they had dinner in a restaurant nearby. Elizabeth went to great lengths not be recognised and so far it seemed to be working.

They both went to bed at 11 o' clock and then in the morning, after a light breakfast, they set out to the car rental shop that was the other side of the quaint friendly city.

It was a sunny morning and Elizabeth was enjoying the walk. The people of the city were going about their daily business without any idea that the heir to the British throne was walking amongst them.

Elizabeth wanted to make a short stop at Cardiff City Hall, as she wanted to see something about this building of which she had read. Turning a corner there it was a fine Edwardian building.

Looking up Elizabeth saw it on top of the main dome, an intricate beautiful if not fierce looking sculpture of a dragon. It seemed to be looking out over the city. Elizabeth thought that it looked so real that it may take to flight at any moment.

Smiling to herself Elizabeth and Cherie walked on to where they hoped to rent a car for a day or two.

Cherie dealt with all the formalities and then within half an hour the two of them were driving out of the city towards Caerphilly, with Elizabeth herself driving. She had told Cherie that she simply wanted to have a look around and it did not take very long to get there. She told her trusted companion to go and have a look at the local shops and that she would be just fine alone for an hour and that they would meet up a little later in that tea shop on the corner.

Elizabeth made her way to the ruined castle, for every path way seemed to lead to it. It was indeed a ruin but if, like her, you use your imagination, you could see it how it was hundreds of years ago:

People coming and going, the battles fought in and around it but now it was an empty shell, an echo of a time when Lords and Earls ruled the land and their word was law. Those days were thankfully long gone and now there was for the most part peace in Britain.

As Elizabeth walked around the deserted ruin she got the distinct impression that she was not alone, and as she walked in to what was once the great hall of the castle she was suddenly startled at the sight of a lady sitting in a low hollow window, A fine looking lady with eyes as blue as the summer sky, with long hair, with a silver ring with a white stone on the second finger of her right hand.

She was smiling at Elizabeth and Elizabeth, getting over the shock, suddenly felt silly because in her heart of hearts she knew that she would be meeting this lady here today. She knew that before the day was out she would come face to face with the same lady she had met that hot day months ago on her 21st birthday, some nine thousand miles away from Wales.

The lady stood up and gave a low curtsy and said, "It is very nice to see you again, Your Royal Highness. Please forgive me, I did not wish to startle you but I am sure you knew that we would meet again?"

Chapter 16
The Promise

Smiling, Elizabeth said, "Yes, lady, in my heart I knew but until I saw you a moment ago I was not…." Elizabeth suddenly stopped talking and the lady again smiled and said, "I quite understand, my dear, and there is no need to say any more, but I would ask you to come with me on a short walk as I wish to show you something." To this Elizabeth said, "Yes, Morgana, I would be happy to take a walk with you and it is too very nice to see you again." The lady only smiled at the use of her name and did not react in any other way at all.

Elizabeth for her part did have a list of questions in her mind that she planned to ask the lady if she ever saw her again, but somehow she already knew most of the answers already, including the burning question of the photograph of her at her birthday party when she was a little girl. She knew as soon as she saw the lady that she was in fact Morgana, the legendary sorceress of old. This was the same lady who lived on the island of Avalon and the very same lady from the story that was in the small box made of wood and metal that indeed was given to her by the very same lady now standing in front of her.

As they walked they talked, and Morgana told Elizabeth that she was known by many other names such as Evanora, Sukie and Allagra, she told her that a great many legends and myths had built up around her for thousands and thousands of years and that she was seen by many to be an evil sorceress.

She told Elizabeth that some of the stories were true and some were not, but there were far more important things to talk about at that moment and Morgana then stopped and looked Elizabeth in the eye and said, "My dear it is very important for you to know that I cannot perform magic. I am no more capable of performing magic spells than you are. I know of course that the story within the box mentions me putting a spell upon the mountain at the request the Pendragon king but that part of the story simply isn't true. The real version of that part of the story is somewhat mundane and unimportant. It is my belief that long ago people would see things or hear things they did not understand and needed magic to explain such things as magic was the best way of doing just that. It is my belief that accusing someone of witchcraft was one of the best ways of getting rid of someone you did not like very much.

"The only power I possess is that of knowledge and a great deal of experience"

Elizabeth remained silent and Morgana went on to say "The only thing that is definite about me and you is that I am a great deal older then you. I know of course that to your eyes I am around 27 or maybe 28 years old, whereas in fact I am almost 9000 years old as you would understand it. I have seen empires rise and fall; I have seen kingdoms and civilisations grow;

I have seen acts of despicable cruelty also I have seen acts of such kindness and compassion they would bring tears to your eyes.

I have met with some of your ancestors, indeed I have spoken with the first Queen Elizabeth and tucked a very young Queen Victoria into bed on a cold night and yes, my dear, I was at your 10th birthday party that day and I have been keeping an eye on you ever since all because of what I am about to tell you and ask of you. You will recall the talk we had the day of your 21st birthday. I told you then that the time would come when you would need to act on what was written on the paper with in that box I gave you. Well, my dear Princess, that day is coming ever closer. The day is coming when the dragon could break free of the mountain." As she said this, Morgana pointed in the direction of a mountain some miles away and said, "A very long time ago I tricked a dragon in to a great pit in that mountain. It was not magic and it was not a spell, although at the time and ever since that is what the people of this land have said, but it is not true. That great beast was put there just before a great battle with the help of the people of this part of Wales as well as its prince, who was killed shortly afterwards.

For century upon century it has slumbered deep within that mountain but I fear that in years to come it will awaken and, as it says in the story, it will take revenge on all Wales. But it will not stop there, it will go on to destroy this entire island and beyond. I have seen with my own eyes what it can do and what it is capable of and you, my dear know of the only way to keep it asleep and that is to display its image across all Wales.

You, like most people, have seen stone dragons all over Wales, some big and some small; they have become decorative things. The good people of this land have forgotten why they are so important, but they are getting less and less. I fear that very soon there will be no images of the dragon left, but in time when you become Queen of this land you will have it within your power to do just that. You, and only you, can do this great and vital task and I ask you my dear to honour the promise you made to me and all your people on your 21st birthday."

Elizabeth, who up until now had not said a word, turned to Morgana and said the words, "I declare before you all, and by that I mean you and all the people of this land, that my whole life whether it be long or short will be devoted to your service. I will, when I am queen, promise to carry out what you have asked of me this day and when I am queen and when it is in my power to do so, I will see that the image of the dragon is displayed right across this land of Wales."

Morgana took both of Elizabeth's hands and looking in to her eyes said, "The day will come when you will become Queen, and I think you will be a fine queen and reign over this land and other lands well into the next century." Smiling she went on and said "I will leave you now, my dear, but we will meet again and should you ever need me I will always be here to assist you, for like you I love this island and its people."

Without another word Morgana turned and walked away.

Elizabeth was left standing on the sunlit path and looking at the mountain and then back at the town with all its comings and goings and knew what she had to do. She had a plan and in time she would see that it was carried out. Elizabeth and her trusted companion Cherie left Wales the next day for London. The months and years passed but Elizabeth never forget about that day in Caerphilly, or the small box that was given to her on her 21st Birthday in South Africa that she keeps safe and hidden away in a secret place in Buckingham Palace; every now and again she would bring it out and read what was inside as a reminder of the solemn promise she made on her 21st birthday.

On the morning of the 20th of November 1947 Elizabeth married her charming prince and then the day came that Elizabeth and her husband set off for a five month tour of the Commonwealth that was to start in Kenya. That tour only lasted six days, for on the 6th of February 1952 her father, the King, died and so Elizabeth became Queen. She returned to London and began a reign that would last longer than any other king or queen that sat on the British throne.

Elizabeth was now Queen and as much as her role was very different to that of the first Queen Elizabeth, she nevertheless took a great deal of interest in the day to day happenings of her country and her people.

She was a hardworking monarch and tried very hard to do her duty as well as her father did before her.

The Queen, for the most part, was loved and respected by all her peoples of the world; a world very different to when Lucan lived in that small house near the sea in South Wales, or our dear Hazel, for the London she knew was long gone, replaced with high-rise buildings and populated with people from all over the world.

As for Mark, he wouldn't recognise his home of Portsmouth or the city of Bath in the 21st-century but things must change and nothing can stay the same forever.

Iris too lived a long and happy life after the war and she too never forget that strange encounter that day in her living room with Lance Corporal Jones but like Mark and Hazel she never really understood the great importance of what she did by simply writing a short few lines of what she considered to be a children's story.

However, Lucan, Hazel, Mark and Iris played their part in preserving their Island home. The four of them were of course the descendants of the four princesses who a very long time ago were made to separate not only for their own safety but the safety of the entire island.

The queen would sit at her desk each morning and a footman would bring to her a red box, inside which were papers and letters from various government offices and departments.

Each day a box would come and each day the Queen would sit at her desk and read each letter and paper. She did not have the power to change or make laws and rules, but she had the right to see what was going on in her country, and so the day came when another box was put on her desk at half past nine in the morning. It was a Tuesday and the Queen had just finished her breakfast and just like every morning she took her place at her desk and opened the box and saw the usual pile of papers and on the very top was an envelope with the letters ER written on it in black ink. Picking it up and opening it she saw it was from a Welsh Member of Parliament.

In the letter the man was talking about how it was high time that Wales had its own flag, and that the Welsh people, although loyal to Her Majesty felt it was time that Wales had a flag that represents them in the world.

The Queen read the letter and then read it again; she knew at once what she had to do. She knew that if there was to be a new Welsh flag for Wales and its people then it had to have upon it a dragon, for what better way to display the image of a dragon across all Wales and in turn see that the dragon forever slept inside the mountain.

So began a great deal of research, both historical and current; a great many ideas, opinions and designs were put forward until finally after many months it was decided that the flag would be similar in appearance to that of the one used by King Henry VII at the battle of Bosworth in the year 1485, it too incorporated the red dragon that was an ancient symbol of Welsh kings and princes. The field of green and white was to represent the House of Tudor and its Welsh dynasty, and maybe also to represent the leek that is also a national symbol of Wales, and so the new Welsh flag came in to being in the year 1959 and very soon it was seen everywhere across Wales and so from that day to this the dragon sleeps inside the mountain. But from time to time someone will hear a rumbling deep in the earth. There will be any number of reasons and explanation given for this but do not forget that some people think that they can pick up a newspaper or put on the television and be told why things are the way they are in our world, they are given an explanation and that's that forever, but the world is not like that.

The years went by and with it came the dawn of the 21st century and the Welsh flag still flies across Wales.

From Cardiff to Snowdonia the red dragon can be seen on a field of white and green.

The Welsh people love the flag, and it continues to inspire Welsh patriotism. People of all ages can be seen waving Welsh flags on rugby match days in Cardiff, and young schoolchildren colour in the flag and proud parents stick it to the fridge at home and there aren't many homes in Wales that do not have at least one interpretation or image of the dragon within its walls.

Could this have been what Morgana had wanted and hoped for? Could this have been her plan all along?

If so then we can assume that she is now content and happy for where ever you go in Wales the dragon can be seen just like the one on the roof of Cardiff City Hall that can be seen guarding the city and capital of Wales in Cardiff. Indeed the Red Dragon has become synonymous with Wales but how many of its people really understand why this is so?

Caerphilly Mountain has now become a local tourist attraction and on a sunny day it makes for a pleasant afternoon walk, but again how many people really know that a dragon is sleeping deep within that mountain? There are still a lot of questions but some of them may never be answered in a rational, satisfactory way.

Chapter 17
The End?

It is March the 1st and spring is on the way.

Daffodils can been seen everywhere across the country, the birds are making nests in the trees and there is a feeling of anticipation in the air as the days are getting longer and the people of this land are looking forward to a long, hot summer that will hopefully follow the spring.

It's a bright but cold Monday morning with a white frost covering the grass on the road side where clumps of even more daffodils can be found.

There is a small church standing just off the road; its graveyard is overgrown and forgotten but some of the words can still even now be made out on the tombstones although the people who were laid to rest there have been long forgotten and it has a feel of abandonment about it.

At the gate there is a woman. She stopped here this morning only out of curiosity and to lay a single daffodil on to each grave, why she did this isn't clear although the daffodil is the national flower of Wales. Could it be that she once knew the people who now rest here or could it be just an act of kindness and remembrance but as we know some times some things just do not have an answer and they like so many things in our world they forever remain a mystery.

She has been this way before but the last time she walked this way this old church was maybe not so old but it has not lost any of it charm and even mystery.

It has been many, many years since this woman has been to this part of south Wales but she considers it part of her island home and as much as she will not be here for very long today she will always return here from time to time to if nothing else than to remember a time when things were not better or worse only different.

She makes her way back on to the main road and needs to take care because it is rush hour and cars are speeding up and down and there is no pavement on this part of the road, but turning left she starts to walk up hill.

The road steps up three times until at last she is standing on a grass verge at the side of the busy road and from there she can look out over a ploughed field and beyond that she can see the coast line and across the sea the English county of Devon.

The last time she came to this very spot a great oak tree stood at the bottom of the field and more or less where she is standing there was a stone house and yard but all of that is long gone and to the rest of the world the man who lived here is long forgotten but to her he was an old friend and she can remember him as clearly as one would remember a childhood friend from years ago and so smiling to herself she continues walking down hill, past a caravan park and in to a small seaside town that she also knew well and it may have changed and been added to over the years, a great deal of it has not changed very much at all and she is very happy to be back here after such a long time.

Today is Saint David's Day and although originally a religious feast day it has also become a day of celebrating all things Welsh, from Welsh culture to Welsh food and Welsh music, poetry and sport.

School girls dress up in traditional Welsh costumes and the boys wear daffodils or leaks and they are photographed for local newspapers.

Welsh cakes are made and there is a feeling of patriotism and history in the air.

The woman is making her way to the centre of town because she is meeting up with an old friend whom she hasn't seen face to face in decades but this meeting will be slightly unusual for her friend is world famous, her name is known by everyone everywhere and it is very important that she isn't recognised by anyone in the town for her stay here in this seaside town will be very brief indeed.

As the woman approaches the main street she looks up and sees bunting, the design of which is very familiar to her and, smiling, she makes herself comfortable on a bench near a bandstand. Within minutes she notices four tall handsome young men walking discreetly up the main street; they do not attract any attention from the townspeople nor does the elderly lady and her companion who are walking in between them.

The elderly lady who is carrying a black handbag approaches the bench smiles and sits down, her companion and the four men take positions around the bench but out of ear shot.

Neither of the women on the bench speaks for several minutes, they just look at each other smiling and each seemed happy in each other's company and then the elderly lady spoke first and said, "Well, Morgana, it has been a very long time but as I sit here with you today I am reminded of the first day we met all those years ago in South Africa."

Morgana smiled and said, "Yes, your Majesty, I was just thinking the same thing!" As she spoke she patted the Queen's hand, and in doing so they both laughed.

There was no awkwardness between them for they were old friends and as they chatted a crowd of schoolchildren came around the corner next to the band stand all holding and waving Welsh flags.

Both ladies looked at each other and smiled.

This was now the end result of a story that started over 9000 years ago but that's not to say it was the end of the story because some say it is just the beginning of something much bigger.

THE END
The end, that is, of this story

A note from Morgana......

It's important to let you know that I have met with people who you would consider fictional, I have met with the person you would call Robin Hood, although this person did not live in Sherwood Forest and did not have a band of merry men, although this person did indeed steal from the rich people of the area and give it to those in need but this person was not a man in fact 'Her' real name was Robyn Hoodwig, she was a disgruntled noblewoman from the north and the name "Hoodwig" was given to her by the people she helped, because from time to time she would disguise herself with a long somewhat shabby homemade wig to avoid being recognised by the authorities.

Robyn did not like the way the poor people were being treated by their overlords and one day she decided to do something about it, she left her comfortable home and her family and went out in to the world,

She to my certain knowledge never used a bow but was an expert with a sword although she did not ever kill anyone. Overtime, however, her reputation was enough that when she decided to steal from someone rich more often than not that person would simply hand over whatever she demanded from them.

She was a great warrior and protector of the poor, she did all she could to fight injustice in this land. I admired her greatly, but of course over the years and after she died a different and somewhat masculine story built up around her deeds to what you would now consider to be common knowledge and her name was changed to Robin Hood because like all old stories good and bad they are changed and retold to suit the beliefs of those who are telling them.

A very long time before I met Robyn Hoodwig I became friends with a woman now considered to be one of Britain's greatest heroines, the spelling and pronunciation of her name has changed over the centuries but you probably know her as Boadicea or Boudicca or indeed here in Wales she is sometimes called Buddug of the ancient Iceni people. The story goes that on the death of her husband he left his lands to both his daughters and the Roman Empire. A short but incredibly barbaric battle broke out between the followers of Boudicca and the Romans - years after the event some Roman writers accused her and her followers of unspeakable atrocities; they claimed that she chose to kill herself instead of being captured by the Romans.

I must tell you that most of that story simply isn't true for I was there and I saw with my own two eyes what really happened and I feel that it is important that you know the truth not for historical accuracy or by any means to destroy what has become a great British legend; a story that has inspired the belief that the people of this country, or anywhere else for that matter, can do anything in the face of adversity. No, I wish to tell you what really happened for you to have a better understanding of how stories change to better fit in with how people wish to see the world.

It all began long before I was given the ring of Silver with the unusual white stone, I was living in what is now called East Anglia in England, it was of course a primitive land and life was hard. I lived in a small hut on the outskirts of a large settlement that was at that time inhabited by the ancient Iceni. They too were just as primitive as their surroundings and like most of the tribes long ago they were warlike and forever in conflict with their neighbours, but there was something different about the Iceni.

Yes violence and conquest was a way of life for them, but there was something else too and that was their ability to tell stories and that is way I settled there in my small hut for a very long time. I got to know Boudicca and her husband Prasutagus, in fact I assisted Boudicca to give birth to her first daughter. It was during this time that the Roman Empire invaded and conquered the vast majority of this island; then, things began to change. Prasutagus made an alliance with the Romans, but it was after his death the trouble began. I saw with my own eyes how how Boudicca and her daughters were treated and yes, there was a rebellion, but it was a peaceful one, Boudicca did not order the burning down of what was then called Londinium, but encouraged the native peoples of that town to join them in peaceful resistance. Unfortunately it was no good and thousands of native Britons including Boudicca were killed. I know that isn't the story that has made its way down the centuries to today, but it is a very good example of how stories, myths and legends can change over time just like the legend of how the Welsh flag came in to being.

I now live happily in Wales; however where I live exactly is not important, but I will say that from my bedroom window I can just see the top of Caerphilly mountain where, thanks to Quintus Arelious, Lucan, Hazel, Mark, Iris, Queen Elizabeth and many others, the great dragon now forever sleeps.

What's left of the land of my birth is just off the coast of Lands End in Cornwall and as much as I do visit there regularly I now call South Wales my home.

The Dragon in the Snow

This short story is about a Welsh town, a school teacher, a mountain and a boy called Kenneth and it takes place over 120 years ago at Christmas in South Wales and what happened that week can still be 'heard' today by anyone who takes the time to listen.

This tale tells us that the very best stories come from those who can speak from experience, not only from being there in person, but from what we are thinking and feeling at the time so we can then put them down in words and they will always be the best of tales and from just a small story anything can happen and it did….

You have met the man who wrote this story and his name was

Sir John Evans

It is dedicated to
Christopher, Nick and Cherie

Chapters…..

1 The Story.

2 The Dragon People.

3 Kenfig Pool.

4 The Dragon.

5 The Visitor.

6 A Walk In The Snow.

7 The Painting.

8 Under The Mountain.

Chapter 1: The Story

Our story begins in South Wales in a town that is over looked by a mountain. It may not be the biggest mountain in the world but a mountain nonetheless.

The snow lay thick on the ground. It is December and Christmas is coming. The year is 1899 and the people are waiting with great enthusiasm to the dawn of a new century.

Although none of us can see into the future we can only hope that things will improve for all of us.

The town in this story isn't that different to any other town in South Wales, it has several public houses, a church or two, shops and houses of all different shapes and sizes, the people who live there are no different to those from any other town in South Wales only there is one exception and that is one member of the community, she is much respected in the town of Caerphilly.

The woman in question lives in an ordinary house, in a ordinary street, she is somewhat tall, but if you were to ever pass her in the street you probably wouldn't even notice she was there but if you did the one thing you would notice would be her eyes for they are it is always said as blue as a summer sky.

Her eyes are of course not the reason this woman is so respected amongst the other towns people no she is much admired because she is one of the kindest and most generous of all the people in Caerphilly, there is very little she would not do to help others in need.

She is known by everyone and she is the most selfless person you could ever wish to meet.

She was known in the town simply as Miss M, and that is how everyone who met her addressed her but if you were to ask anyone in Caerphilly what her first name was I doubt very much if anyone could tell you.

Miss M, looked to be about 28 or 29 years old but no one knew when her birthday was.

She was a teacher in a local junior school in the town.

The children in her class loved her and each and every one of them looked forward to Friday afternoons for it was then that their teacher would tell them a story.

Her stories were legendary in the small school and they were full of adventure and mystery, of ancient peoples and faraway places, of knights, Queens and great battles and dragons.

Each child would every Friday afternoon sit and listen in wonder to their beloved school teachers' exciting stories.

So it came to the last week of the school year and all the children were excited and very much looking forward to the Christmas holidays that would begin in just three days time and then after the Christmas holidays were over they would return to school not only in a new year but it would be the start of a new century, the 20th century and there was a feeling of great optimism not only in Wales but in the rest of Great Britain too.

The school children made their way to the old school building through the snow on a very cold Wednesday morning. Some had their Mams with them and some a little older perhaps are allowed to walk to school alone or with their friends.

Every house in the town had smoke coming out of their chimneys and the smoke hung heavy in the air on that cold morning. The smell of burning coal could not be escaped by anyone who happened to be walking around the town on that cold morning.

Each child would have to walk past the great ruin of a castle that stood in the middle of the town. Its ancient walls looked black against the cold Iron grey sky.

Each child walking to school that morning knew that the castle was built in around 1275 and of its resident ghost the Green Lady of Caerphilly Castle. She was said to be a heartbroken noblewoman who walks the castle grounds late at night in search of her lost sweetheart and that is why no self-respecting resident of the town would be seen in the castle grounds after dark.

There were of course other myths and legends connected with the area, for example there was the myth of the mountain, an ancient legend that told how meany hundreds of years ago a group of travellers made camp on the top of Caerphilly mountain and during the night were awoken by the sound of what could only be described as snoring coming from deep within the Mountain.

Over time the noise that those people heard was attributed to an even older story that told of a great monster asleep deep within the mountain. Indeed some of the very same Children walking to school that morning would come running down the mountainside claiming that she or he had heard the beast snoring deep within the earth!

But today the children's thoughts were not on ghosts and monsters but on Christmas and presents.

As usual the headmistress of the school was waiting at the gate for the children to arrive, she was a strict but very kind lady and seeing that each and every child had safely arrived she closed the gate to the play ground and ushered all the children inside through a heavy oak door in to the old stone building.

The school day always began with an assembly, that is to say all the children and teachers would gather in the school hall for prayers and to sing the national anthems and then the children would separate into their respective classes to begin lessons for the day.

As the children took their seats in Miss M's class room they opened their desks and brought out their exercise books and pencils.

Miss M, greeted them in Welsh as she usually did and with a smile she began to tell them what lessons she had planned for them that day.

In the afternoon there would be two hours dedicated to mathematics and some time would be taken concentrating on multiplication, she ignored the looks on the children's faces, she knew of course that most of the children in her class just like most children then and now find such things rather boring but the morning would be she hoped a little more fun and interesting.

She began by asking the children what their favourite school experience was from the last year and while doing so she intended to ask each child to write a story about it.

A boy who sat in the front row of desks put his hand up and said "Miss my favourite was the time we went on a day trip to Porthcawl" and the girl next to him said that her favourite lesson was when they learned about Llandaff Cathedral in Cardiff and then at the back of the class a boy called Kenneth put his hand up and said, "Miss my favourite is every Friday afternoon when you tell us a story" to this the rest of the class nodded in agreement for each and all of them enjoyed their teachers stories.

Miss M, looked a little surprised because this boy who always sat at the back of the room didn't speak out very often in class, he was shy yet intelligent, but for whatever reason he didn't show how much he knew. He was rather tall for his age, he had short brown hair and green eyes with freckles on his nose.

Kenneth was popular enough with his classmates and had friends in school but he liked to spend a lot of time alone. He wasn't very good and didn't much like rugby or other sports, but he loved books and above all he loved history, that above all things in school was his favourite subject.

He was fascinated by stories of kings and queens, he loved to hear stories of everyday people in ancient times, he also loved myths and legends and the stories that Miss M, would tell every Friday afternoon fascinated him.

Miss M, then asked the class to write out exactly what they enjoyed the most from that year in school and then asked the children to explain why they enjoyed it so much and what it was about their experience they liked so much.

Chapter 2: The Dragon People

The morning went by and at a quarter to twelve the bell rang and it was time for lunch, all the children stood up and made their way to the door but not before placing their exercise books on their teachers' desk.

When the last child left the room and closed the door behind her Miss M, picked up the first exercise book off the top of the pile on her desk, sitting down she began to read, the book belonged to Kenneth, the boy who was sitting at the back of the class. Taking the book and sitting at her desk she began to read and by the end she felt very special and appreciated for every word was dedicated to the stories that she told her class every week, there was even a short list of his favourite stories....

> **The Dragon From Across The Sea.**
> **The Prince and the Dragon.**
> **The Dragon and the Ring.**
> **The Dragon from the black forest.**
> **The Dragon of Three Step hill.**

Miss M, didn't have to be a genius to work out that Kenneth's favourite stories were the ones she told about dragons, she of course told other stories about all kinds of other things such as stories about when the Roman Empire ruled most of Britain and stories of tyrannical rulers of Wales a very long time ago but it would seem that this boy enjoyed stories of dragons and Miss M, decided that because it was Christmas and on Friday it would be the last day of term her story would be about a dragon.

The next few days passed with a feel of Christmas in the air, the children made Christmas cards for their Mams and Dads, there was a Christmas concert and a very nice time had by all and then on Friday afternoon after lunch Miss M asked the children to push their chairs and desks to the side of the room and sit on the floor on a large rug in the middle of the room.

Miss M, took her own chair from behind her desk and placed it in front of the children, she then sat down and began her story in the time honoured way of any story teller...

"Once upon a time"

A very long time ago on an island the people called Albion there lived a group of people who referred to themselves as ***Vir et mulier in draco*** and loosely translated it meant The Dragon People, this somewhat peculiar name came from an ancient legend told amongst them that had been passed down through the ages. It told of how a small group of nomadic people came to Albion from across the sea in a boat that they had made especially for the journey, on board there were men, women and children, they were all looking and hoping to make a home for themselves and moreover to explore this new and somewhat different land.

The name Dragon People it is said came from the fact that each of them had around their necks on a piece of string a small clay model of a dragon that, if legends are to be believed, this small talisman or amulet would give them some protection should a dragon ever attack them or their settlement, why or how this worked remains a mystery.

The legend also tells that on board the rickety vessel were two other passengers, a woman and a man who were not part of the nomadic group but did spend time with them in their home land before they even reached their destination and went a long way in persuading the nomads to travel to this new land to the north.

It was said that not long after their arrival on the shores of Albion they separated, the group of nomads headed north past the great white cliffs and deep in to what would become their home and their descendants would in time become strong and prosperous.

Nothing is known of what became of the two other passengers, where they went or what they did is not mentioned in the legend however as the years turned into decades and into centuries strange stories were told of a wise woman from across the sea who seemed to have the power to heal the sick with little more than a mixture of herbs.

It was even said that this woman never grow old and had the power to live forever but those stories were for the most part sketchy and sporadic. There was even a story that this woman would sometimes travel to and from the legendary kingdom of Lyonesse but they were probably just myths for Lyonesse is a place routed in mystery and if it did exist it certainly doesn't anymore.

Could this woman be the same woman who arrived on the beaches of Albion with the nomadic dragon people? If it were true then this woman would be a great age by the time the stories surrounding her began to circulate.

There too were stories of a man who lived in the far north of the island who it is said never seemed to grow old and would spend his days alone in a small hut writing out stories in what became a book that over time became the property of a prince, could this be the other passenger on the boat? Again they were only stories and rumours.

Chapter 3: Kenfig Pool

In the classroom the children were sitting in silence, this wasn't anything new of course because the children were always mesmerised by their teacher's stories.

Each child did not want the story to end for isn't it true to say that when it comes to all great stories we never want them to end, yet getting to the end and knowing the outcome whether it be good or bad, happy or not is what we really want. How many of us have wished at the end of a good book that we hadn't read it at all so we could have the pleasure of reading it for the first time and isn't that the signature of a good story?

Miss M, went on and told the children that The Dragon People after leaving their boat and the two passengers at the seashore headed inland, they were used to travelling around, they were hard working and didn't let little things like a new island and a strange and different landscape bother them.

Of course there were other people living on Albion but for the most part the new-comers lived in peaceful coexistence with the native peoples for centuries and over time with the introduction of farming it meant that the nomads, known by everyone else as the dragon people from across the sea, began to settle in one place.

Some travelled to the west and some to the north and east but the biggest settlement was established in Searoburg in what is now known as Salisbury. Just like their native neighbours they established a belief system that centred around the changing seasons, the landscape and even the stars; so came the day that a great circle or Henge of stones was erected and became the local centre of spiritual belief. For century upon century they stood as a testament to those people who came to the land of Albion in a small boat long ago and those great stones still stand more or less in the same place.

The descendants of those Dragon people who left the original group and travelled west came to a land that was truly beautiful, a land of mountains and rivers, of great ancient forests and vast sandy beaches.

They too prospered and were known by the local people as '*Pobl y Ddraig o Gymru*' which in the ancient Welsh language meant simply 'Dragon People from Wales' again this was because of the small clay models of Dragons they wore around their necks that were not unlike those that belonged to their ancestors.

Their stories told of how long, long ago a fearsome dragon threatened their native land beyond the sea and it was said that just showing its image would repel this terrifying beast but nobody really knew why or how.

The Dragon People from Wales eventually settled on the coast and established a small but thriving settlement, its people were the first to settle in this particular area and in doing so they quite literally laid the foundations of what is now the town of Porthcawl.

Miss M, smiled when she noticed a grin on the face of the boy who just days ago wrote an essay in his exercise book that told of his visit with the rest of his class earlier that year to the sea side town of Porthcawl. She too remembered it very well, it was a lovely day and the children were very excited about being at the seaside, there were buckets and spades, sandcastles and ice creams for all.

Miss M, and another schoolteacher a Mr Evans spent the day with the children in Porthcawl and on that particular day Miss M, got the opportunity to have some time to herself.

It was customary on school day trips such as this that two school teachers would be in attendance and it was understood that one of the teachers in attendance would have the opportunity to get three to four hours to themselves and it was the turn of Miss M, to do just that.

On other occasions such as this when the teacher got the opportunity to have some time alone they would generally go off and sit in a tea room or even a pub but Miss M, didn't have any intention of doing ether, no she had for some time now wanted to visit a place not to far way called Kenfig.

Miss M, set out on foot along the coast past Rest Bay and across the sand dunes until in the distance she could just make out a lake that was completely surrounded with sand dunes.

There was a great many myths and legends connected with this pool of water in fact the local people called it Kenfig Pool.

It was said that long ago a small town once stood here but over time the sand began to cover the town and as legend would have it one night during a terrifying storm a great rush of water from the sea engulfed the town and all that was left was a great pool of water!

It was said that the bell of the church can still be heard during stormy nights deep in the middle of the pool!

Indeed the entire area had a strange atmosphere. There was evidence to indicate that humans lived in the area as long ago as five thousand years. The Romans too settled here for a time and when they left the Danes known as Vikings began raiding the area, they came from across the sea in their longboats decorated with images of Dragons!

Then in time came the Normans who maintained a permanent settlement in the area.

So it could be said that this area had always been occupied but with several different peoples some of which came from different parts of Europe, so it isn't unreasonable to think that the area would give off a feeling of history and legend.

Chapter 4: The Dragon

Miss M, made her way up and down the sand dunes until finally she reached the edge of the pool, she had wanted to visit here for many years having read about it in many different books and now finally she had made it and it was everything she expected it to be and more.

Miss M, knew that this place hadn't changed very much in hundreds of years and it was quite obvious that few people visited this place.

There was something else about this place that an old friend had told her long ago when Porthcawl was a very different place. It was from a time when it was a strong independent town but its people where not warriors or soldiers but artists and poets and they lived in peace with each other.

When in the distant past this fine town actually existed isn't clear and most of the evidence of this thriving town cannot be found but if you know where to look you can sometimes find a clue to a past that cannot easily be explained away and like all stories and legends there is always a grain of truth to them.

The sun was now high in the sky and Insects were buzzing and flying around in the long grass nearby, an adder made its way silently past looking for an excluded spot to bask in the midday sun.

There were any number of birds in the cloudless blue sky and Miss M, was just standing at the water's edge looking out over the pool, in the distance a beautiful white swan was gliding effortlessly across the water.

She closed her eyes and in her mind she recalled the story of a man who once told her about the day he sat down some where here at the pools' edge long ago to take a rest from his journey home, what this man witnessed or so he said was nothing short of terrifying. If her old friend was to be believed and Miss M, had very little reason to doubt him the tired traveller saw a DRAGON! And what made this story even more unusual was the fact that Miss M, believed every word of it.

Now we all know that dragons do not exist do we not? They are simply works of fiction and stories of them come from a time when people believed in all manner of creatures that we know never existed outside of fantasy such as unicorns and goblins and the like? However it could be argued quite reasonably that the stories of dragons are not quite as mythical as we would first suppose.

Imagine if you would an average human being two or three thousand years ago, he is digging a hole, maybe he is looking for water to build a well or perhaps he wants to bury something precious to him and in doing so he comes across the fossilised remains of an ancient creature that we would now call a dinosaur. He has never seen this creature before, it is completely alien to him and it is nothing like the animals he can see around him.

This is something very new and he cannot explain it, he doesn't have the knowledge that we have today, he doesn't understand that these creatures were wiped off the face of the earth millions of years ago, he doesn't understand that the bones he has found are fossilised, he has absolutely no idea that this animal died millions of years ago and so the only way to explain this discovery is to build a story around it to better explain and indeed understand.

Could it be that there was a great storm at the coast that battered some cliffs and exposed the fossilised remains of say an animal such as a fossilised Tyrannosaurus Rex! Again the people who saw such a thing wouldn't know that this animal died long ago and it's reasonable to believe that because of these ancient fossilised creatures the stories of dragons came about.

I think it would be important in this case to stop and ask yourself this question, from the photographs and images you have seen of dinosaurs do they look that different to the photographs and images of dragons you have seen?

Perhaps Miss M. asked herself that question that hot sunny day over 120 years ago as she stood looking out over Kenfig pool.

She didn't however stay very long and after only around ten minutes she started out on the walk back to Porthcawl and the children.

Did she visit Kenfig pool that day out of simple curiosity or did she visit because she wanted to see for herself where a very long time ago a man saw a dragon fly over the lake and disappear in to the distance. Maybe she just wanted inspiration for one of her stories that she would tell her class every Friday afternoon. Was it the inspiration for the very story she was right in the middle of telling her class on that Friday afternoon just before Christmas?

Chapter 5: The Visitor

In the classroom a cold afternoon December sun was shining through the high windows and the children's eyes were fixed on Miss M.

So far in her story she had told the children about a group of people who had made their home by the sea in what is now Porthcawl. She went on and told them that as the years passed the population got bigger and the Dragon People from Wales became rich and powerful but they used their power and wealth for good and they traded goods such as wool and bread with other parts of South Wales.

They saw that each child had the ability to hunt and take care of her and him self from a very young age.

Although they were not war like each townsman was required to complete a year of military service.

This requirement was just for men although woman also had their part to play and as such every woman over the age of twenty was required to practice at least once a week with a sword.

She told the children that not very much was known about the town or what went on there from one day to the next but what was known was that it was made up of four areas or districts each with its own leader know as Princeps who were elected by the people of their district each year to speak for them and each week the four Princeps would meet and discuss any problems or issues that may have cropped up.

They discussed all manner of issues from the distribution of food to the rules around land boundaries.

They also did something else that was essential but not always easy to carry out. The four Princeps also acted as judges and would enforce the laws of the town but they did so with an eye to mercy, justice and compassion and it had been that way for as long as anyone could remember.

The four Princeps would meet at precisely midday and this week it was the turn of the northern district to host the meeting and so it was the four of them, that is to say three men and one woman took their places at the table.

The table was circular in shape and an exact replica sat in each of the other three great halls in the other three districts of the town.

The great halls were little more than long huts with a thatched roof and walls made of straw and mud and the outside had been painted white.

The meeting started in the usual way with each of the Princeps standing up and reciting the motto of the town leaders which in English was...

We the representatives of the dragon people of South Wales will to the best of our ability serve the people of this town with honour and dedication and to the best of our ability cause justice in mercy and forever strive to earn the trust of those whom we serve.

Then it was to business, only today all other business was to be put to one side for today something different was going to happen, today someone was coming to meet with the four Princeps, this wasn't that unusual for the townspeople often came to make requests or to hear a judgement, but today the visitor wasn't a member of the town, no, she didn't even live in South Wales; in fact no one really knew where she lived or what her name was but she had made a request to address the Princeps and in turn it was granted and so at precisely midday the door to the great hall opened and all four of the Princeps got to their feet and there in the door way stood a tall woman, her eyes even in the dim light of the great hall seemed to shine a bright blue, her hair was long and fell down her back. She was wearing a simple yet elegant blue robe that was drawn in at the waist with a brown leather belt that at first glance seemed to be decorated with the images of some kind of winged animal and she was holding a long wooden staff.

The lady gave a small curtsy and thanked them for allowing her to visit. What she had to say came as a shock to the Princeps, the lady told them that she wanted to warn them of a great army who were at this very moment advancing all across Albion, they were from a land fair away across the sea, they were a mighty fighting force and countless settlements were being destroyed! She told them that they should at once fortify the town and prepared for invasion!

To all of this news there came a torrent of questions from the Princeps...

Who are you!? What is your name!?

Where exactly did this army come from?

Why are you here telling us this?

You are not one of us!

Are you a spy?

The atmosphere in the great hall became extremely tense but the lady remained calm and did her best to answer all of the questions that were being thrown at her.

She told them that she was a friend of all the peoples of Albion and she was doing her best to visit all the settlements she could to warn them of what was coming! She told them that she lived in the hills far away to the north and that one day the news of this invasion army reached her.

As for the name of this force it was THE ROMAN ARMY and as we now know this army invaded, conquered and occupied most of what we would call Britain.

As for her name, most of us know it and she is part of our mythological history, indeed this lady's name can be found in books and even on television programmes nowadays,

Indeed every child sitting in Miss M's class room knows her name.

She is known because of her role in the ancient stories of King Arthur and Camelot but in that small town in South Wales a very long time ago nobody had ever heard of MORGANA

Chapter 6: A Walk In The Snow

In the classroom every child gasped! Two or three of them even clapped! They were all surprised and excited to hear that Morgana was part of the story! They, of course knew of her! They felt extremely excited about this and were all smiling, all that is except the shy boy Kenneth.

The look on his face could only be described as intense suspicion, his eyes were fixed on Miss M, and for a moment their eyes met and within that smallest of moments Kenneth came to a profound realisation, but only being a child he really didn't understand it, he didn't understand what he knew to be true and for today at least he didn't act on it.

Miss M, looking down at her watch suddenly realised that it was almost half past three and it was time for the children to go home! Their Mams would at this very moment be gathering at the playground gate to collect their children to take them home! And so for the first time ever Miss M did not have time to finish her Friday afternoon story. After wishing them all a very Happy Charismas She told the children to quickly gather up their belongings and get ready to leave. The children seemed a little disappointed for not hearing the end of the story but the Christmas holidays were about to begin and Miss M, assured them that she would finish her story after the holidays. All the children began to line up at the door in preparation to leave but Kenneth seemed to be taking a long time getting his things together and he was still looking for his ruler by the time all the other children had left the classroom. Miss M didn't notice him at first because she too was busy putting her things into her bag.

Kenneth gave a little cough and Miss M. turned around and she wasn't in the least bit surprised to see Kenneth standing there alone in the class room and before he could speak Miss M, smiled and said, "Kenneth I have been thinking, would you like to hear the rest of my story?" To this Kenneth nodded with enthusiasm because of course that is exactly what he was going to ask her but he wasn't prepared for what came next..

"Very well, I will call at your house at 1 o'clock on Christmas Eve and we will go for a walk, I have no doubt whatever that your dear mother will have any issue with this and I will write a short note now before you leave for you to give to her to explain that I will be calling on Christmas Eve to take you out for a walk." Kenneth was extremely excited and asked Miss M if she would tell him the rest of the story when they went on their walk and she said she would, but she told Kenneth to dress warmly and their walk would no doubt take them out of the town.

By the time Kenneth got home it was getting dark. He gave the note to his Mam and as Miss M, predicted she did not see any problem with Kenneth going out for a walk on Christmas Eve with his school teacher for Miss M, was regarded with a great deal of trust and admiration in the town.

Kenneth for his part was looking forward to Christmas Eve partly because he wanted to hear the rest of the story and because he knew that by the time their walk was over he would better understand what was at the moment just a jumble of thoughts and ideas in his mind.

Three days later at precisely 1 o'clock in the afternoon there came a knock at the door of number 86 White Street and standing on the door step was Miss M, she was dressed in black boots, a long black skirt and a heavy woollen black coat, hat and gloves. She was also holding a long stick the kind that had a V type fork at the top where the bearer could place their thumb.

She was all set for a cold walk in the snow on a crisp day with the sun shining and a thick layer of snow on the ground.

She did not have to wait for very long on the door step and within less than two minutes the door opened and Kenneth was standing there in a woolly bobble hat, a scarf and his coat was fastened tightly against the cold.

They both cheerfully greeted each other and set out on their walk.

Miss M, did not speak for some time but Kenneth was keen to know where exactly they were going and give some suggestions to where they could take their walk that afternoon.

He suggested they go and see the Christmas tree that had been erected in the town centre or maybe take a walk around Caerphilly Castle but as they walked down the street Miss M, smiling looked at Kenneth and said "My dear boy I think you know already where we are going" Kenneth just laughed and said "Yes, yes I do"

It was of course obvious where they would be going that afternoon and it was as if Kenneth already knew but for whatever reason he didn't want to say.

As they made their way out of the town in the direction of Caerphilly Mountain Miss M, asked Kenneth if he would like to hear the rest of the story and of course her young companion was very keen indeed to hear it, he knew that by the end of the story he would not be quite the same again.

Chapter 7: The Painting

Miss M, picked up the story from when Morgana was talking with the Princeps, she went on and told of how after three or four days they finely conceded to her advice and put in to place the emergency plans that had long been in a state of readiness in case of invasion or some other disaster. Each of the Princeps coordinated these plans in their respective districts and Morgana would travel to each district and offer help and assistance where it was needed.

It was during her visit to the southern district of the town that she met a man who for all his eccentricities seemed somehow completely sincere.

He was known in the town as an Artist–come-Historian-come-Storyteller, he was completely harmless but had the reputation of being rather short tempered and preferred to be alone most of the time. He lived in a large dwelling that was more or less on the beach and one day having heard that Morgana was visiting he sent word to her and invited her to his house by the sea.

It seemed that he was excited at the prospect of having someone new in the town and someone who didn't necessarily find him odd or strange.

He was of late middle age with a rather misshapen bushy beard and like all the residents of the town he had around his neck on a piece of string a small clay model of a dragon.

The sun was setting by the time Morgana reached his house and he was standing in the door way smiling at her as she approached. He suddenly became very excited and invited her inside. He offered her food and drink and began asking her all kinds of questions but did not seem very interested in her answers and then he finally asked her in to the next room where on one of the entire walls of the room was a giant painting and at once Morgana knew that this was the precise reason he invited her here!

The sole reason for the invitation was this painting and it was sadly obvious that no one else apart from himself had ever seen it. Maybe the other townspeople just weren't interested or he just didn't want anyone else to see it but he was extremely proud of it and he had good reason to be for it was truly magnificent.

It was almost dark but he had expertly arranged candles in the room so that the painting could be clearly seen and the flickering light of the candles give the painting a dramatic edge.

Morgana was taken aback and could not take her eyes off it. The man was quite literally shaking with excitement and pride!

The painting was of a lake surrounded by sand dunes with the sea in the distance and above the lake was.... A Great Red Dragon in flight! The detail of this animal was truly extraordinary! Its eyes were as black as pitch! Every red scale could be seen on its body!

Its tail was long with a spike at its end; it had strong legs with great feet and black claws! Its wings were stretched out and resembled those of a bat but were red in colour!

Morgana, pulling her eyes away from the painting and looking at the man said, "Sir this painting is truly magnificent! Could it be that you have painted this from memory?"

Something inside her knew that this man had seen this great flying beast and he had gone to a great deal of trouble to immortalise it!

Smiling modestly he turned to Morgana and rather quietly just said, "Yes I have seen it, I have seen a Dragon and I fancy it's the very same one that my ancient ancestors came to this land to escape from centuries ago! I saw this beast not quite three years ago when I was resting next to a large pool of water about four miles from here!

And you lady have seen this animal before haven't you? I know because I have seen what is engraved on your belt! I know that you are the same lady who travelled here to this land with my ancestors a very long time ago!"

Morgana didn't see any reason to deny it; every word this man had said was completely true! She was the same woman and she had seen the dragon! She was a great age and some would even go so far as to call her immortal!

To her certain knowledge there was only one other of her kind that she knew of and that of course was the man who like her travelled to this land of Albion with the dragon people from across the sea centuries ago!

How this man who created this fine painting was in possession of this knowledge was unclear but his house wasn't just full of paintings no it was also full of ancient looking books and we may suppose that he came by this knowledge within one of them? But who knows.

Chapter 8: Under The Mountain

Miss M, and Kenneth were by now at the foot of Caerphilly mountain, almost an hour had passed and it was time to rest before the gentle uphill climb to the top of the mountain or so that is what Kenneth thought. The two of them settled themselves on a bench that was free of snow because it had been protected by a low over hanging tree. It was very cold but they were very well dressed up against the weather.

Kenneth spoke first; he had lots of questions, such as, "What happened to the town and the people when the Romans came?" and "where did Morgana go and if she is immortal where is she now?"

Miss M, smiled and told Kenneth that the Romans did indeed come to the town and for a time it was very difficult but as the years passed both the townspeople and the Romans learned to live together in some kind of peace and although Roman culture and ways of doing things finally took over and the town was eventually absorbed into the Roman Empire of Britannia the people did not suffer.

As for the question he asked on the whereabouts of Morgana, there wasn't any answer Miss M, could give because he already knew where this mythological lady was, he already knew that this legendary lady was at that very moment sitting next to him on that bench.

Miss M didn't say a word she just smiled at Kenneth and said, "My dear boy I have something to show you, but before I do it is very important that you know that as long as you do exactly what I say no harm will come to you, for there is nothing, absolutely nothing, that can hurt you" Kenneth nodded in agreement and asked Miss M, if he could for the remainder of their outing call her by her real name of Morgana, to this she agreed and standing up she walked behind the bench they were sitting on, got down on to her knees and cleared the snow from a patch of grass and then to Kenneth's astonishment she began to peel back a section of grass to reveal a wooden door that was flat to the ground with an old Iron ring in the middle of it.

With the greatest of ease she pulled on the Iron ring and the wooden door came away leaving a square hole in its place.

Morgana reached inside and pulled out an ancient looking lantern and after lighting a candle that was inside it with a cigarette lighter she just happen to have in her pocket she jumped inside the hole and out of sight!

Kenneth by now was both excited and terrified; he was actually in the presence of a woman that up until last week he always thought was little more than a fairy story! And now he was about to follow this very same woman into a hole in the ground! And that is exactly what he did! As he jumped in his feet hit the frozen ground beneath and to his further astonishment Magana was standing up right in front of him in what looked like a long tunnel!

Putting her index finger to her lips she indicated to Kenneth that she wanted him to follow her. She raised the lantern high on the V stick she had brought with her so they could both see where they were going. Neither of them spoke and time did not seem to exist down here in what seemed to be an ancient tunnel.

On and on they walked until suddenly Morgana stopped turned and whispered the following words into Kenneth's ear, "It is very important you do not make a sound"

And then taking Kenneth by the hand they turned a corner in the tunnel and what came next was absolutely unbelievable! There in an enormous cavern the size of a Cathedral was a giant mass that was making a sound that could only be described as snoring! Kenneth couldn't make out what it was at first but of course he knew what it was, he knew that this 'Mass' was nothing more than a dragon!

There wasn't time to study this creature anymore because Morgana took hold of Kenneth's hand and pulled him back around the corner and back all the way through the tunnel and up and out of the hole behind the bench and she didn't speak until the wooden door was back in place and the grass was rolled back over it.

Morgana indicated to Kenneth to sit on the bench and she sat next to him, for his part he was in a semi state of shock but he soon came to his senses when Morgana said "My boy I want to tell you a story" to this Kenneth became excited because he knew that this story would go a very long way indeed in explaining why and indeed how this enormous dragon ended up deep inside a Mountain in South Wales!

Again Morgana started with the time honoured words "Once upon a time" there was a Prince who began to worry about a dragon he had seen fly across his kingdom! He was a good and brave man and he was loved by his people!

One day he went to seek advice from a wise woman who lived in the shadow of this Mountain in South Wales, she was more than happy to offer advice and practical support to his problem. After much hard work the Prince, his family and all his people, not to mention the wise woman, managed to trick the dragon into the mountain through a great pit that the people of all Wales worked together to dig. There it went to sleep and after that the years went by and a great deal changed; the wise woman, however, found it necessary every one hundred years to check on the slumbering dragon and did so every Christmas Eve.

She checked on it to make sure it still slept deep within the mountain!

"Are you the wise woman?!" Asked Kenneth his voice high and excited.

Morgana smiling just said "Yes I was and I was born a little over 9000 years ago and I have seen this world change in countless ways" she went on and told Kenneth that she would be leaving South Wales soon but not just yet. She also told him that it was important that he never tell anyone of the door under the grass behind the bench but she did ask that in the years to come he share her stories for stories are so important.

Christmas came and went and all the children including Kenneth went back to school and Miss M, as promised told the children the rest of the story but only Kenneth knew that it wasn't a fairy tale, myth or legend! He knew that it really happened and it was from memory not imagination and years later when Kenneth was around 39 years old he wrote a book that was inspired by what he had been told and what he had seen during that White Christmas when he was a little boy, his book was called **THE DRAGON ON THE FLAG**. He was very proud of it and his hope was that the day would come when everyone just like you would get the opportunity to read it.

The End

About the author

Paul Harries-Holt was born in 1980 and spent most of his growing up years in the seaside town of Porthcawl in South Wales some 40 miles west along the cost from the Welsh Capital of Cardiff.

When he was a child he loved to hear stories, myths and legends and his late father would take him and his younger brother on long walks and it was on these walks he became interested in local history as well as the countryside and the coast.

He enjoyed beach combing on hot sunny days or walking miles to visit a ruined castle with his very own walking stick that was cut, preserved and given to him over 30 years ago by his Dad.

He was and still is also fascinated by British history and all of this has been the inspiration for this book not to mention the truly inspiring history and landscape of South Wales and other places in the United Kingdom.

From tales of smugglers at the coast and the legends associated with the churchyard at Newton in Porthcawl and from Ogmore to Cardiff to the Brecon Beacons Paul has absorbed the atmosphere of this ancient land and this book came together because of how much he loves not only South Wales but all of the United Kingdom.

He now lives and works full time in Cardiff with his partner Nick and his cat Monty and can be found wondering around museums and Art galleries in his spare time.

The Dragon on the flag is his first book however a second is in the Pipeline but the title of that story is for the moment a secret!

Printed in Great Britain
by Amazon